SECOND
FIDDLE

Or How to Tell a Blackbird

from a Sausage

SECOND FIDDLE

Or How to Tell a Blackbird from a Sausage

Siobhán Parkinson

ROARING BROOK PRESS

NEW MILFORD, CONNECTICUT

Published by Roaring Brook Press
Roaring Brook Press is a division of Holtzbrinck Publishing Holdings Limited
Partnership
143 West Street, New Milford, Connecticut 06776
First published in the United Kingdom in 2006 by Puffin Books, London

Distributed in Canada by H.B. Fenn and Company, Ltd.

Library of Congress Cataloging-in-Publication Data
Parkinson, Siobhán.
Second fiddle / Siobhán Parkinson.—1st American ed.
p. cm.
Summary: Outspoken Mags decides to help her new friend Gillian,
a talented violin student, reconcile with her estranged father so that he will allow her
to attend a prestigious music school in England.
ISBN-13: 978-1-59643-122-5
ISBN-10: 1-59643-122-9
[1. Violin—Fiction. 2. Fathers—Fiction. 3. Divorce—Fiction.
4. Death—Fiction. 5. Ireland—Fiction.] I. Title.
PZ7.P23935Se 2007
[Fic]—dc22 2006019924

Roaring Brook Press books are available for special promotions and premiums.
For details, contact: Director of Special Markets, Holtzbrick Publishers

Book design by Jennifer Browne
First American Edition April 2007
Printed in the United States of America
2 4 6 8 10 9 7 5 3 1

To Shannen, Sophie, Shauna, Samantha, and Deirdre,
who taught me the importance of finding lost fathers,
and to the Cashell family, especially Sophie,
who does not remotely resemble any of the characters here.

AUTHOR'S NOTE

If you are wondering what the title of this book means, you will have to read on, and by the end you might understand, though I am not making any promises. The reason it has two titles is so that it can't possibly be mistaken for any other book of a similar title, though people tell me this is not likely. Also, I like books and stories that have two titles. It gives you a choice, and I am all for choice. It has a democratic feeling to it, don't you agree?

Signed: *Mags Clarke*,
Author

A False Start

This story is mainly about me. It was going to be mainly about Gillian, but I have to admit that, when it comes down to it, I find me more interesting. There is quite a lot about Gillian too—only sometimes I forget and call her Miranda, by the way, which I hope you don't find too confusing; I've tried to get it right most of the time—and without her, there wouldn't be anything much to tell at all, but still, if I am honest, which I usually am, it is largely about me.

I have read some fairly hair-raising stories about kids my age, with all sorts of stuff in them like divorce and bullying and drugs and discovering you are gay and cancer and anorexia and puberty and alcohol and all that jazz. These things do happen, of course, and I think it's a good thing that you can read about them in books, so you will know how you are supposed to react if you ever have to deal with them in real life, only I do think that in some books, an awful lot of dreadful things happen to the same one or two people, which doesn't seem all that very believable to me, if I am honest, which I am most of the time, but I think I told you that already.

Just so you know what to expect, there is a little bit of divorce in this book, and one small occurrence of death too, only I don't really go into the details much, so it's nothing to be alarmed about. And there are pretty well none of the other things I mentioned that you get in those other realistic novels. I say "other" because this is a realistic novel too: it is about ordinary life and real people, with no ghosts or dwarfs or wicked counts or Gothic castles or anything like that.

I have heard that it is very important to have an intriguing opening when you are writing a story, so I thought for a long time and I came up with what I think is a fairly intriguing opening to my story, and I will tell you what it is in a minute. But first, here's a reader warning: I am planning to be a writer when I grow up, and I am going to use this story to practice a few little phrases that might be a bit sophisticated. I promise it won't get too heavy or bothersome, and anyway you don't have to read it if you don't want to (though I hope you do, of course). Also, I do find that people (tiresome people, mainly) say it is good for you to learn new things. Your teacher, for example, would probably say that. Teachers love burrowing in books for long and difficult and especially new words that they can make you look up in the dictionary. All those teachers can't be wrong, can they, so, I suppose it must be good for you to learn new things. Sometimes teachers don't even notice the story or the funny bits, they are so busy making you learn new words. I think the best thing is to give them a few new words to keep them quiet while the rest of us get on with enjoying the story, but also I like new words myself, so they aren't just there to keep the teachers happy, if I am honest, which . . . oh no, I think you know that bit.

There may be the odd poetic sentence here and there as well. I don't put these in to annoy you, but you do need to have a bit of atmosphere in a story, you know. I hope my more discerning readers will put up with the poetic bits and the occasional long word, because if nobody reads my story, I will feel rather bad about that, and I am only twelve after all, so you might have the ordinary decency to read my first stumbling efforts. Twelve is a difficult age for a girl, and I might be scarred for life.

Anyway, I've thought a lot about intriguing openings, and in case anyone reading this is looking for an intriguing way to start a story of their own, I can let you have a few ideas I thought of but didn't use, so they are to spare. But I won't bore you with them now. You can send me a letter and ask me if you want. I won't charge, which is a pretty good deal, because most people these days charge for advice, don't they? Anyway, this is my intriguing opening, more or less:

The forest was the last place you'd expect to see such a thing. It—I mean, she—was a strange girl, with a brown cloud of hair, and she was standing right there, apparently suspended in the leafy air, high

*above the woodland path, practicing. When I squinted, I could make
out that she wasn't suspended in midair after all—*

One reason she was not suspended in midair, by the way,
is that that is contrary to the laws of nature and this is not
the kind of story where weird stuff happens. This is as
weird as it gets, more or less. I myself like books where the
laws of nature are broken, it's just that this isn't one of
them. If that is the kind of book you like best, I can recommend the writings of Ms. JKR. (I can't say any more,
for copyright reasons.) Or if you like truly weird and very
funny, there are always the books of Mr. LS (not his real
name). But the main reason she was not suspended in
midair is that—we're back in the story now, keep up!—*she
was standing on something quite solid*, and if you read the next
chapter, you'll find out what it was.

I would like you to know that I have worked very hard
to make this opening as intriguing as I could. These things
don't just arrive all by themselves on the page. Somebody
has to do a lot of thinking to make things as interesting as
possible for the people who are going to be reading the
story. Especially in this kind of book, where there is no
magic or heroic deeds or flying cars or slaying of dragons
or shooting with guns. And by the way, in case any boys
are reading this, I should add that there is absolutely no
football. There is a boy, but he is nicer than most boys,
mainly because he is nearly grown up and consequently

not as jumpy as other boys. If you are the kind of boy who is prejudiced against books with girls in them, well I feel sorry for you.

And finally, you might take note of the fact that I did not begin this book by saying, "My name is Mags Clarke." A lot of people do that, and it is not very interesting, so if you want a hint about writing, that is my first piece of advice to you: avoid beginning by telling people what your name is. This is also not a very good way to begin a letter, by the way, because of course most people put their name at the bottom of a letter, and any halfway intelligent recipient of a letter knows to look there if they want to find out who is writing to them.

I think I will have to begin again now, because all my explanations have gotten a bit mixed up with the actual story, and you might be confused because you are not as well versed in the story as I am, and you may not be as clever either, but of course I don't know you, so I could be wrong about that.

A Fresh Start

The forest was the last place you'd expect to see such a thing. When I thought about it afterward, trying to remember, there was this dreamy feeling to it, as if maybe I hadn't seen it after all, but I know I did, because later, I got to talk to it—I mean to her. She was a girl with a brown cloud of hair, and she was standing right there, apparently suspended in the leafy air, high above the woodland path, with her back to me and her elbow out, practicing. An unknown girl playing the fiddle in the forest.

When I looked again, I could make out that she wasn't suspended in midair after all, but was standing on something quite solid: the balcony of a tiny wooden hut, which was so well hidden among the trees that I had never noticed its existence before.

"There worn't no 'ut 'ere yestern," I muttered to myself in the special woodland voice I'd invented to go with my new persona as a girl who has made the woods her territory. I shook my head as well, in the sorrowful sort of way that I thought best suited the woodland voice: a slow, shaggy shake that made my hair swing. I was enjoying being a woodlander. (You might have noticed that yourself, but at the beginning of a story, I thought it might be helpful to nudge you along a bit, just till you get used to it.)

Nobody contradicted my muttered observation, which is the great thing about being alone in the woods—or nearly alone, but of course, the girl with the violin was too far away and too engrossed in her music to hear what I told myself under my breath. We were all alone together in the forest, except for the trees. It made me go all shivery when I thought of it like that. It seemed spookier than being all alone by myself, if you see what I mean.

"Not ver' frien'ly, iz she?" I said to myself as I studied the strange girl's back.

I could see the creamy top part of her back and the top two or three knobs of her vertebrae because she was wearing one of those boob tube shirts with no shoulders; you know, the kind shaped like a large sock with the foot part cut off, which just goes down over your body and sort of sticks on by itself—elasticated, with no straps or anything to hold it up. Not—I should perhaps make it plain, since of course you don't know me very well yet—the kind of garment I am given to wearing myself.

I snorted without really meaning to. It was the elasticated top that did it. It seemed such a silly thing to be wearing in the woods.

The girl must have heard me, because she suddenly stopped playing.

I stood absolutely still and concentrated on my head-breathing. In case you don't know what that is, it's when you close your mouth tight and breathe very lightly and softly, so that it feels as if your lungs are hardly involved at all, and the spaces in your skull seem to fill silently with air instead.

Perhaps the girl was only taking a "rest." That's what you call it when you don't play for a note or two. I know that because I was in the choir at my old school, in the second alto line. "Rests" are anything but restful. They just give you time to imagine how dreadful it would sound if you hit a wrong note when it is your turn to start up again.

The girl with the creamy shoulders seemed to be having an extra-long rest. She stood there, with the violin clamped between her shoulder and her chin, her elbows poised like awkward wings, while I tried to make myself invisible and inaudible and breathe only in my skull, which gets a bit stressful after a time, you may as well know in case you want to try it for yourself. I thought the girl must be listening, because I could see that her head made tiny movements, and I noticed that the movements slunk down the side of her body and came out at her right foot, which tapped out a slow rhythm.

I watched the silent violinist's back for maybe half a minute, and then suddenly her elbow started sawing again and she played a final violent burst, leaning dangerously far over on her left side so that it looked as if she might topple over the flimsy wooden railing that ran around the porch. At the last moment she straightened up, flung one arm out from her body, and made a low, sweeping bow to an imaginary audience.

I laughed, because all I could see of the bow was the girl's bottom sticking up, gleaming synthetically in tight-fitting Lycra leggings, and the top half of her body disappearing below the rail of the balcony. There she goes, bum in the air, big black shiny peach—if she could see herself from this point of view!

The girl spun around at the sound of laughter, but I stepped quickly backward into the greenery. I knew that there was nothing to be seen where I had stood, except perhaps the uncanny nodding of the long, protective arms of the brambly brushwood that hid me from view.

Gillian

I don't spook easily, but it was a bit eerie. I could have sworn that someone laughed, and when I turned round, the brushwood was nodding, as if someone had just stepped back into it.

I told myself it was probably a squirrel making the branches wobble, or a wood pigeon, great big clumsy things. They go plodding around on twigs that are too small to bear their weight. It's a wonder you don't find more of them with their necks broken on the forest floor.

That's all it was, probably, just the local wildlife getting a bit restless. Maybe they think I am some kind of extraordinary new bird. The fiddler-bird.

Note to the Reader

The bits called "Gillian" in this story are where Gillian butts in, but of course, even though she is talking, I have actually written those bits too, because I am the author of the whole story. The thing is, though, I am not Gillian, I am Mags, so I don't actually know what Gillian was thinking at any point. I do know her side of it, roughly, because she has told me so that I could write it down to make the story, but obviously, I have had to make up her actual thoughts, and don't for one moment imagine it is easy.

I have tried to make Gillian sound like herself, which is sort of bossy and remote, and not like me, which is friendly and amusing and clever, but I don't know if it is working all the time. Sometimes my own voice might slip out, like a ventriloquist having a bad day. But I promise to do my best not only to give her side of the story, to the best of my knowledge, but also to be fair to her. That is not always easy, since she is not as interesting a person as I am, though of course she is very talented in her own way, and most of the time she is perfectly pleasant to be around, though at other times she is insufferable. But I try to paint her in as kindly a light as I can.

Mags

"Foresters' hut," my grandfather said when I called by his cottage on my way home that evening. He was pouring half a bottle of tonic water into a glass. He always drinks tonic at five o'clock, with a slice of lemon and two ice cubes clinking in it. He calls it his "sundowner." He smirks when he uses that word, as if he has said something terribly witty. I gave a dutiful grin and said "Sláinte," which is what you are supposed to say when Grandpa makes his sundowner joke.

"They keep their tools in it," he went on. "Their jackets too, and their teapot and gas ring for the cuppa tea in the mornings. You can't beat a cuppa tea first thing."

I was disappointed that Grandpa was so matter-of-fact about my story of the strange girl and the funny little hut that had just seemed to appear out of nowhere. I wasn't sure exactly what a forester was, beyond a vague idea that it was the modern word for "woodcutter." In stories, woodcutters tend to be poor men whose wives long to have babies. This didn't seem right somehow.

"Could a girl be a forester?" I asked.

"You could do worse," said my grandfather, misunderstanding me completely. Typical of adults. "Nowadays, anyone can be anything they like, can't they? Though I wouldn't tell your mother, if I were you. She has her heart set on you going to university."

"What heart?" I asked bitterly, kicking the underside of my grandfather's chair with the toe of my sandal. Sometimes I'm a bit hard on my mother, I suppose, but it works both ways. (By the end of the book, as you will see if you make it that far, we are getting along together much better. I know that is a bit of a cliché, and that in most books people who are at loggerheads at the beginning end up being all pally at the end, but I can't do anything about that because it's true; that's how it turned out. Sometimes life is more like books than you expect it to be.)

"Ah, Mags! You know your mother loves you."

"Only because she has no choice," I said. "She'd stop if she knew how."

"That's nonsense. She thinks the world of you."

It wasn't nonsense in my view. I hate to have to admit it, but I am a disappointment to my mother. My mother would have preferred a daughter like the girl with the violin, one who'd wear a shirt like a surgical corset, a confident girl with talent and probably friends, who could stand up in front of an audience and who definitely doesn't spend her time mooching about the woods getting herself muddy. I don't get myself muddy on purpose to annoy my mother, if that's what you're thinking. It's just that if you muck about in the woods, mud happens. My mother doesn't seem to understand that.

"She'd love me more if I was a Miranda," I said, polishing an apple I'd filched from the kitchen on the ribbing of my jumper.

"A Miranda?" said my grandfather. "Who's Miranda when she's at home?"

"Oh, nobody. Just a girl."

"Miranda, she's called?"

"Naw, that bit's not true," I said, biting into my apple with a satisfyingly loud crunch. "The name I made up."

"But not the person?"

I swallowed my bite of apple too quickly and it made cornery progress down my gullet. "Only the name," I said, swallowing extra saliva to wash the lump of apple down. "I had to make the name up because I don't know what she's called. I haven't met her. I only saw her back."

"You only saw her back. But you know enough about her to think your mother would prefer her to you. Oh, Mags!"

He's always saying "Oh, Mags!" Come to think of it, a lot of people are always saying "Oh, Mags!" as if I were some sort of troublesome puppy. I'm not troublesome in the slightest. I don't see why people think they have to throw their eyes up about me all the time.

"Yemp. That's about the size of it, Gramps."

I took a swig from my grandfather's glass, to chase the cornery bit of apple down. He rolled his eyes.

"Don't call me Gramps," he grumbled. "I'm not some old American codger. And don't drink my gin."

"Y'are so an old codger." I bit into the apple again, hard. "Anyways, it's not gin. You can't fool me."

"Of course it's gin," he said with mock grumpiness. Sometimes he does mock grumpiness so well I wonder if it's not real grumpiness. "And I'm Irish."

"Well then," I said, crunching carelessly.

"You are a *difficult* child, do you know that, Mags Clarke?"

"Hmph. Yemp."

"And you shouldn't eat with your mouth full."

I laughed, revealing a mouthful of half-chewed apple. He doesn't mind that sort of thing, because he is an old codger. It drives my mother wild.

Gillian

There is definitely someone hanging about the woods. She looks a bit like something the cat brought in, with her scruffy clothes and her hair all rats' tails around her shoulders, like a Neanderthal. There's a new family over the other side, someone said. She must be part of it. New people are usually better, because they haven't known you all their life; they don't think you couldn't possibly amount to anything because they always knew your grandfather was a terrible farmer and as for that hopeless creature your father married, poor man. . . . Well, of course, she *is* hopeless, but that isn't the point.

Goodness knows, I didn't choose for this to be the one thing I'm any good at. If I had a special gift for making apple tarts or hairdressing, I'd make apple tarts or cut hair till the cows came home. I wish I could. I'd like to work in a bank when I grow up, or open a coffee shop or set up a Montessori school, and then people would say, "Hasn't she done well? Considering everything. You have to admire her spirit." They like you to have spirit, but in manageable amounts, and you also have to use it in approved ways.

(I don't think Gillian would be capable of constructing this sentence, actually, but I have to give her adult-sounding things to say from time to time because she is a bit older than I am. You can't just introduce a person and say, "She is a year and a half older than me," even if it's true, because that is too obvious. You have to have the satisfaction of picking up some things for yourself. Signed: *Mags*)

Mags

I saw Miranda again in the woods a few days later. She was just coming out onto the porch of the foresters' hut. I was watching from behind the brambles, and on a sudden impulse I stepped forward and called up to her. I don't know why I did it, because I definitely didn't like the idea of this hut, this girl, all this activity in my forest.

It isn't really a forest. It's only a scrap of woodland on the hillside, but I forested it with my dreams. (Sometimes I write down interesting ways of saying things, like this, in a notebook, but then I usually lose the notebook, so if, like me, you are planning to be a writer when you grow up, I don't really recommend it as a writing technique, unless of course you are more organized than I am. I didn't get this sentence in my notebook, because of course my notebook is lost. It just came to me as I was writing the story down. You can call it inspiration if you like. I call it just being good at writing.) I had a sort of a den in a clearing by the stream, and there I could Sherwood to my heart's content. There was a smooth slab of slaty stone that made a good table, and I kept my water bottle cooling in the running river.

"Hallo!" I called, stepping firmly out of the brambly undergrowth. "Hallo there! Hi!"

The girl looked around, startled, clutching her walnut-colored violin by the neck. She made a sunshade over her eyes with her hand and peered into the greenery, searching for the source of the voice—me, in other words.

"I'm Mags," I shouted up. "I live over yonder." I'd never used the word *yonder* before. It was part of my woodland vocabulary. I wondered if I was pronouncing it properly. "Who're you?"

"Gillian." The girl's voice was high and precise. A soprano, no doubt. Altos and sopranos never get along; it's a well-known fact, like Scorpios and Geminis.

"Suits you," I said. There weren't many names that were worse than "Miranda," but "Gillian" definitely was.

Gillian tossed her cloud of hair. She'd located me by now on the woodland path below her hut.

"So does yours," she shouted down to me. "Suit you. Mags. You're a Mags all right."

I wasn't sure that this was friendly information, but Gillian followed it with an invitation. "Come on up. My brother's just making the tea. You can have a cup if you don't mind powdered milk. We've got Kit Kats too. Only the fun size, though."

I nodded. Wasn't it just typical of someone like Gillian to invite me for *tea*? Only grown-ups ever offer people tea. She looked older than me, but not very much older. I hoped she wasn't going to be all big-sisterish.

"Stairs are over this side," Gillian called, pointing around the side of the hut.

I followed the direction she pointed in and found that rough wooden steps, made out of cross sections of tree trunk, had been fitted at uneven intervals into the sloping bank. Clever, I thought, picking my way carefully from step to step. You'd hardly notice them, if you weren't looking for them.

"When I was small," Gillian announced as I arrived on the porch, "my brother told me the woodland fairies had made the steps and disguised them so human beings wouldn't notice them. I believed him, because it's true the hut is very well hidden. I don't know why people wanted to disguise it."

"Fairies, huh?" I said, careful to use my woodland voice.

I noticed that Gillian's face was too small for her neck and her eyes were not of an interesting color. That was something, anyway.

"Well, I was only small," Gillian said.

"Well then," I said in a slightly apologetic tone. Apparently I say this a lot. I haven't noticed it myself, but people keep imitating me doing it, so I suppose it must be true, and for this reason, I drop it into the dialogue from time to time to give an authentic flavor. That's a good tip, by the way, if you are interested in writing. Give your character a catchphrase.

"Come in," said Miranda. Gillian, I mean. The way her little head bobs on her long neck, and those pale eyes—pure Gillian.

"This is my brother, Tim," said Gillian. "Tim, this is Mags. She lives, er, over yonder."

Tim wasn't what you'd expect of a brother. That is to say, he seemed almost grown up. More like an uncle. And tall, like a tree, with his brown-haired head a very long way from his elbows, which is about where I reached to.

"We're new," I said helpfully. "We moved in last month. What's the story with the violin?" I sat down on a paint-stained chair that Gillian pointed out.

She handed me a mug of tea. It was strong and hot. The powdered milk formed curdy lumps in it and did nothing to cool it down. I stirred but the lumps wouldn't dissolve.

"It's for making music on," said Gillian's brother. His voice boomed above my head.

"Well, of course it is," I said, to Gillian rather than to Tim. His ears were so far up I felt I'd have to shout to talk to him. "I *know* what a violin is. I mean, how come you play it, and why *here*?"

"I play it because . . . ," Gillian began pertly. Then she stopped. "I don't know why I play it." She gave her brown cloud of hair another little toss.

Lord preserve me from soulful persons! I bet she practices that toss of her head in the mirror.

There was only one Kit Kat left, I noticed, in the rectangular lunch box they used as a sort of biscuit tin. But I was the visitor after all. Surely they'd offer it to me—they'd have to, if they had any manners.

"Have a Kit Kat," Gillian said, as if she'd heard me thinking. She offered me the almost empty box. She wore nail polish, I noticed, the see-through kind, no color. It made her fingers seem even smaller and pearlier than they were naturally. My mother wouldn't dream of letting me wear nail polish. Not that I had ever wanted to.

"Well then," I said, taking the Kit Kat casually, as if there were dozens of them left. "But in the woods," I went on. "Playing a violin in the woods. It seems strange. You'd think it would get . . . oh, warped or something."

"Warped?" Gillian seemed puzzled by this idea.

I gave up on her. She struck me as not too bright.

"Why don't you sit down?" I said to Tim.

"Because there are only two chairs," he said. It seemed he'd heard me, in spite of the long-distance ears. I love that about Tim. He always answers exactly the question you ask, even if it's not quite the question you mean.

"Well then," I said.

That was true, about the chairs. It wasn't exactly what you could call furnished, the foresters' hut. It was full, but not furnished. The two chairs and the table weren't even all in the same place. The table had a jar of teabags and a gas ring on it and a bottle of gas under it, and was at the back of the hut, under a tiny, cobweb-festooned window.

One chair was plonked at random in about the middle of the room. Gillian sat on that. My chair was near the door. You couldn't easily move the chairs, as there was so much junk on the floor.

Of course, it mightn't be junk if you were a forester. Coils of rope, tools, sacks of things tied with twine, dirty plastic bags bulging with nails and screws, piles of jackets and ragged pullovers, metal bars, bright hard hats looking a bit like fireman dress-ups from a toy box, and everywhere, resinous piles of wood shavings and sawdust. (You should look up *resinous* if you don't know what it means, because I will be using it quite a lot since it is very apt for a book set partly in a forest. It isn't all set in the forest, by the way, in case you are getting tired of leaves and trees and things.)

I thought about offering Tim my chair. I'd rather he sat down and I stood up. That way we'd be about level and I could look at him and have a conversation. But he might think that was peculiar, so I didn't in the end.

"You mean, does it go out of tune?" said Gillian.

I looked back at Gillian. "Do I?" I said. I couldn't remember what we'd been talking about. And then I remembered about the violin. How it didn't seem to get warped in the woods. Yes, I suppose that was what I had meant—that it might go out of tune.

I expected that Gillian would tell me it *did* go out of tune, actually, and then go on to explain what she did to counteract that, or that it didn't, as a matter of fact.

But Gillian didn't say either of those things. Instead, she put her mug down carefully at her feet, between two sawdust hillocks, and picked up the violin from where she'd laid it in its open case on one of the piles of jackets. The inside of the violin case was lined with red silk. It reminded me of the lining on a cloak that had belonged to a magician who'd performed at a birthday party when I was small.

"Shall I play for you?" Gillian asked shyly. She was fingering the wood of the violin as if it were a pet that needed comfort and reassurance.

I couldn't remember what it had sounded like last time Gillian had played, but it couldn't have been too bad, because I'd have remembered if it had been terrible.

"Hmph," I said, remembering my woodland voice again all of a sudden. "Yemp."

It was terrible. Truly terrible. Like a sick cat. I listened in horror as Gillian drew dreadful squawks from the strings. Her too-small face was all screwed up with concentration. She looked as if she was in pain. I certainly was. No wonder she had to play out in the woods where she couldn't upset the neighbors!

Suddenly Gillian stopped. "Right," she said. "What'll I play?"

"Hmph," I said. "What was that? What you just played there now, the first thing?"

"Nothing. I was only tuning up."

"Oh," I said. "Hmph."

Gillian laughed. "You didn't think that was *music!*"

" 'Sall the same to me," I said grumpily. " 'Sjust noise."

It wasn't true. I can hold a tune as well as the next person. I used to be in the choir in my old school. Oh, I think I told you that already.

"No, it isn't," said Gillian. "Listen to this. It's a blackbird."

She stood up and went out onto the porch.

"I can't play in there," she called through the open door. "Too stuffy, it makes the music go all limp. Now, listen. It's a blackbird, I think."

Then she picked up her bow and did that listening thing again, just like the other day, only this time I could see her face. She'd closed her eyes so you didn't have to think how pale and uninteresting they were, and her whole face was dreamy, creamy, hardly like a face at all, more like a picture of a face, all the features perfectly aligned and perfectly at rest. Her eyebrows made perfect arches. I hadn't noticed that before. And her head didn't look too small when she cradled it into the violin.

I hardly heard when the music started. I could see the bow moving over the strings, but the sound was so soft, it was barely audible. Then gradually it began to swell and drift in from the porch and fill the dark and resinous little hut with melody.

Suddenly the music stopped. I opened my eyes. I hadn't realized I'd closed them.

" 'Snot a blackbird," I said at last in my woodland voice.

"I never 'eard a blackbird that sounded like that there."

"No, you're not following me." Well, that part was true enough. Gillian's face looked small again, and bland, now that she'd taken the violin from her shoulder. She was like the overlooked mousy person in an Agatha Christie story who turns out to be the murderer. My mother has dozens of those books and I read them when I run out of library books. "I don't mean it sounds like a blackbird *sounds*. It sounds like a *blackbird*."

Of course I didn't follow. How could I? *It doesn't sound like a blackbird sounds, but it sounds like a blackbird.* That doesn't make sense.

"It doesn't sound like a blackbird *sounds*," Gillian said again. "It sounds like a blackbird *being* a blackbird. Listen again."

She settled the instrument back in the hollow of her collarbone and played. Her bow glided over the strings, her eyebrows disappeared under her hair, her elbow almost scraped the floor.

"Well then," I said, and then I listened. I closed my eyes again and concentrated.

And the blackbird—the blackbird swooped out of the trees, sailed right over the hut, and came to rest on the railing beside Gillian. Even with my eyes closed, I could see it, and something happened in my heart. I didn't know there could be a connection between your ears and your heart, but I was sure, quite sure, that something moved in there, something I hadn't known was there at all.

Gillian

That woodland creature, the girl who hangs around the woods—she looks as if she's waiting for the hunter-gatherers to come home and throw her a bone. But the odd thing is, she *got* the music. Kids never get it. My mother says it's because they haven't got the training, their ears are ruined by rap and hip-hop, and maybe that is true, but even grown-ups hardly ever get it. They clap politely because they know that's what they're supposed to do, but you always know it's hollow. But this scruffy Mags creature—she really *heard* it. It was like being showered with sunlight, watching her getting it. It was like watching something becoming human.

Mags

"What's this about some girl you met in the woods?" my mother wanted to know. She tried to sound casual, but I knew she was interested. My mother is always on the look-out for friends for me. It worries her that I spend so much time alone. Parents these days, I have noticed, think it is important for their children to be sociable. Something has changed since those books I like to read, where parents thought that packing their children off to grim boarding schools or to forbidding mansions on the Yorkshire moors with no friends or toys, or leaving them with cruel aunts who beat them and made them eat lumpy porridge, was an OK thing to do. I sometimes think I would have preferred to be a child in the olden days. It sounds like more fun, although also a bit scary, especially the porridge part.

My mother was knitting a cardigan for the new baby. Lemon, in case it was a girl and wouldn't like blue, or a boy, who would be permanently damaged if he wore pink.

"White would work too," I said, fingering the wool, "or green. Mint green, only very pale; it goes with babies' skin. Or lavender."

"You're changing the subject, Mags." My mother managed to make changing the subject sound like a minor crime.

It wasn't our baby. It was a neighbor's.

"What was the subject? Oh yes, Mira— I mean, Gillian. Isn't that a terrible name?"

"No," said my mother.

"You always disagree with me," I said sulkily.

"*You* always disagree with *me*," countered my mother with a sigh. Under her breath, she went on with her endless murmuration: "Knit one, purl one, knit one, slip one, knit one, pass the slipped stitch over the knit stitch, knit one. . . ."

"Nobody knits these days," I said. "Especially not at breakfast."

"Well, I must be nobody then," my mother said, with that little nod she always gives when she thinks she's made a point particularly well. "Purl one, knit one, slip one. . . ."

"She plays the violin," I said. "She's good."

"Hmm?" said my mother, pulling the slipped one over the knit one, always a tricky bit. "That's nice." Trying to sound casual again.

"But her face is too small," I said.

My mother raised her eyebrows but didn't say anything, because she was counting under her breath. Her needles clicked comfortably.

"She's got a brother," I added. "He's a forester. He's very tall."

My mother turned her knitting and began again from the other end.

"I always thought you should take music lessons," she said. "It was your father who said you didn't have to if you didn't want to. You can blame him."

I knew she didn't really mean that, about blaming my father, but it seems to me that being dead puts him at an unfair disadvantage, and my mother shouldn't say things like that. He died just over a year ago. My mother and I had rattled about in our house afterward. At least, that's what my mother always said: *We're rattling around in that house.* People told her not to make any rash decisions, do nothing for the first year, but as soon as the year was up, she sold the rattly old house that I had loved and we'd packed up and come to live near my grandfather, and that's how we got to be here. To make it more like a family. I think that was the plan. Only Grandpa is being contrary, wanting to go on living in his dingy little cottage. He doesn't like the airy bungalow my mother chose, all large windows and views. He says it makes him feel as if he is on TV all the time. I can see his point. I don't much like it either. So we live in our house and he lives in his, and it isn't any more like a family than it was before, except that Grandpa lives nearby.

I sometimes wonder if dead people have special powers, like angels, and can read your mind. That is a spooky idea. Don't have this idea in the middle of the night if you can help it. Especially not if you are thinking angry thoughts about the person who might have the special powers. Sometimes I am very angry with my dad for not being there. It's all right to be angry. The bereavement counselor told me that, apparently, it's all part of what they call the "grieving process." But it doesn't make that nice pat kind of sense in the dark for some reason. In the daytime, when things always seem less terrifying than at night, I try to compensate by thinking only nice thoughts about him. I hope he does the mind-reading thing in the daytime as well.

"Maybe you should have made me," I said now, meaning about the music lessons. "I wish I loved something the way Gillian loves her violin."

"Oh, I'm sure you do," my mother said, in that vaguely reassuring way mothers do that especially irritates their daughters.

"Like what?" I asked, curling my lip. You read that in books, about people curling their lip, and it sounds a bit unlikely, but I have practiced it and I can do it pretty well now, though it is more a wave than a curl, I have to say. Still, you can't say "waving my lip," as that sounds ridiculous.

"Hmm?" said my mother again. She stopped knitting for a moment and put her knitting needle in her ear.

If I did that, she'd murder me. She'd tell me I was going to skewer my brain or something. But grown-ups can do what they like, can't they? Up to a point, I mean. Don't try this at home, by the way. I will not be liable if you skewer your brain. You have been warned.

"Sausages," she said, after a moment's thought.

She took the knitting needle out of her ear, gave the point a little wipe with her fingertips, and went on knitting, thinking that she had answered my question satisfactorily.

I sighed. Maybe she was right. Maybe there are just two kinds of people in the world: people who love the violin and lead beautiful lives and can make blackbirds swoop over woodland huts, and stodgy sausage-eaters who can only stare in wonder at the blackbirds and go back to chewing the gristly bits.

"I'm going to the woods," I announced, standing up. "*If* you have no objection," I added sarcastically, though my mother never gets sarcasm, ever.

"Well," she said, "as long as you're careful. You know I worry when you wander around by yourself. I wish you'd join the Girl Guides or something."

"Mother! Read my lips: I—don't—want—to—be—a—Girl—Guide. I'm not a joiner. I'm a lone wolf."

"OK." My mother sighed. I could practically hear her thinking, *Little Red Riding Hood, more like.* "Make sure your mobile's charged, won't you?"

"Yes, Mother," I said, and I sighed too.

No violin girl today, I noted, as I passed under the stand of trees among which the foresters' hut perched. Saturday.

So, I had the forest to myself, the way I liked it, full of nothing except itself. I put my arms over my head and contorted my body into a delicious stretch. I had my lunch with me. I could spend all day here if I wanted to. It was a delightful, luxurious thought, though I hadn't decided yet exactly what I was going to do with the day. I stretched again and flung my arms out and gave a little skip. That probably sounds a bit soupy, but if you are on your own in the forest, you can do that sort of thing. The thing is not to let anyone see you at it.

Still, I did sort of, just . . . wonder, when I saw the padlock at a stiff angle against the door. I mean, don't get me wrong, I wasn't *lonely* or anything, or *wishing* to see them, but I just wondered, in an idle-curiosity sort of way, where Gillian was today, where her brother was, whether there were any other foresters to open up the hut and make the tea, and whether being Saturday was what made the difference.

Oh well, I thought, the Kit Kats are all eaten now anyway, so what's to care about?

The fronds of silverweed gleamed underfoot on the woodland path under the hut, here and there spattered with the yellow glimmer of flowers. As I mooched along, fists in my pockets, I heard a movement among the tree roots: a rat maybe, or a squirrel. I stopped to watch. The scrabbling sound continued. I held my breath, waiting for the creature to emerge from the shifting undergrowth. The longer I stood, the closer I listened, the louder the sounds seemed to get. I thought I would surely hear breathing if only I listened closely enough. I peered toward the rustling, expecting a small mammal to scoot out of a pile of last autumn's leaves at any moment.

A tiny sycamore sapling rose half a foot out of the browny moving ground and waved young leaves that were barely green. I peered harder. Then I saw it, partly hidden by the baby sycamore. It wasn't a squirrel or a rat, but a bird, a black one, sleek, with an orange beak, heaving and hauling at something from beneath a stone. The bird pulled again and a worm came pink and wriggling out of the earth. The bird swallowed, the worm wriggled, the bird swallowed again, the worm disappeared. Then the bird looked right at me, its eyes beady and intelligent, as if it knew me. I scarcely dared to breathe, but I gave a shadow of a nod, as if in greeting. The bird hopped on both feet, stretched its wings, flapped them, and suddenly it was gone from me with a flurry and a whop, gone to a perch high out of my vision. I thought I got a warm whiff of birdwing, beneath the tang of pine and sap and the fresh woodland air, but I probably imagined it.

I turned away, and then I saw that there was a figure ahead of me on the woodland path, tall and spiky, like a tree in oilskins. Tim. He was waiting for me. I waved.

"Gillian couldn't come today," he said as I drew up alongside him, though I hadn't asked. "She's had news."

"Ye-ers?" I said, in my woodland voice, anxious not to appear too interested, though of course I was. You can't help it, can you? If someone mentions "news," it is always curiosity-making. This is a good tip, by the way, if you are writing a story. You mention "news" and then you string it out interminably before you reveal to your reader what the news is.

"Good news. She said, if I saw you, to tell you to come over to the house, if you're free."

I wasn't sure yet if I was free.

"I mean, *ask* you," Tim corrected himself. "If you'd like to. It's sausages for lunch."

I fingered the sandwich in my raincoat pocket. I love tuna, but it felt suddenly flabby and slithery and unattractive in its clingfilm skin.

"Well then," I said.

"Do you *like* sausages?" Tim asked.

"They're all right," I said. "Do you?"

"They're all right," he said, careful to give nothing away.

"What kind of good news?" I asked.

"She'd rather tell you herself. She said to say the blackbird is on the wing." He gave a little wink.

My heart gave a funny thump when he said that.

"I know," I said. "I saw him."

"Oh, I don't think she means an actual blackbird," said Tim. "It's like 'The eagle has landed.'"

"I see," I said, though I didn't, not really. "Where's your house?"

"I'll show you," said Tim.

He walked on ahead of me for a bit, following the gra-
dient of the woodland path as it skirted the mountainside
on which the forest grew. The path got narrower as I fell
in behind, keeping Tim's yellow jacket always in view.
After a few hundred meters of a climb, he turned off the
path, in among the trees. I followed. He stopped under an
old oak and turned to me.

"Climb to that bough there," he said, pointing up into
the tree.

"Do you live in a tree house?" I asked.

"Not exactly."

"Well then," I said, and climbed up to the place he had
pointed out.

"Now," called Tim—I was higher up than him now—
"look out that way." He pointed again.

I was still half expecting a tree house, or even a cottage
deep in the woods, but he was pointing out of the forest,
toward a sprawling housing estate, all white and red in the
sunshine, like a Lego town.

"There?" I asked, peering down at him. It was strange
to be able to see the top of his head. "In that sort of
townie place?"

"Yes," said Tim. "If you go straight downward from
here, you'll come to a stile at the edge of the woods; go
over the stile, across that field, then two more fields—no
stiles, you have to get through some barbed wire in the
first, just find a gap in the hedge in the second, it's easy

enough—and you come out just below our house. It's
number twenty-seven, Oak Glade."

"Oak Glade?" I said, coming down from my perch in
the tree. "I see what you mean, that it's not exactly a tree
house—sounds like a tree house but isn't." I laughed.
Or an air-freshener, but I didn't say that part. I am not
entirely tactless, you know.

Tim laughed too.

"Are you *sure* you don't love sausages?" I asked.

"I do," Tim admitted. "I love them."

"I thought you might," I said. I just knew he was one
of us.

"But I can't come with you," he said. "I have to work.
Are you going to go?"

"Oh, yes," I said, just then realizing I'd had every intention all along of going. It wasn't just because of the
sausages. "Here," I added, and I thrust a cold, smooth
little parcel at him. "It's tuna."

"Next best to sausages," he said with a grin. "Thanks."

He shrugged a good-bye and I waved.

After I'd watched him trudge off down the hillside, I
turned to go in the direction he'd pointed me in. The gra-
dient of the hill was quite sharp here. I had to keep digging my heels into the rooty forest floor to keep myself
from sliding headlong. I found the stile all right and
crossed the fields to the outskirts of Legoville. Oak Glade
was the first cul-de-sac. There were houses on one side

only, facing a brambly ditch. Number 27 was on the corner.

I peered at my reflection in the shiny brass letterbox flap. It was like looking at a creature underwater, not much use to tell if my hair was mussed (more mussed than usual, that is) or my face streaked. I took out a tissue and rubbed my nose and cheeks with it, just in case. The reflection in the letterbox flap looked just the same, goldy and watery. I felt my hair-parting with the fingers of both hands and smoothed the hair down around it. Then I knocked.

Gillian

Honestly, she's only half-civilized. She was kicking the doorstep when I opened the door to her.

"What are you doing?" I asked.

"Sorry," she mumbled. "'Sjust a bitta mud. Won't hurt."

She kicked even harder at the doorstep.

"Take them off," I said. I couldn't have her clodhopping all over my mother's carpet in her muddy shoes. "You can leave them on the porch. Do you want to borrow a pair of slippers?"

"No," she said, crouching down to unknot her shoelaces. "Yes," she added, when she saw the state of her socks.

I went and got her my slippers. They're very pretty, pointy-toed mules, in rose pink, flower-embroidered satin. My mother gave them to me for Christmas. She goes in for theatrical presents.

Mags

They were like something out of *Ali Baba and the Forty Thieves*, and they were too big, but at least they hid my shamefully poking toes.

"Who's there, Gillian?" came a voice in dulcet tones from somewhere inside the house. You often hear people using that expression, but this really was like the voice the word *dulcet* was invented to describe.

"It's Mags," Gillian called over her shoulder. "I told you. I invited her to lunch."

"Lunch!" came the disembodied voice again. "But we haven't got any food in."

"We have sausages," Gillian called, "and French bread and that seedy mustard."

"That's not lunch," complained the dulcet voice, "that's picnic food."

I giggled.

"Tell her you love sausages," Gillian hissed to me.

"Who?" I asked. I felt a bit silly about addressing a voice belonging to someone I couldn't see.

"My mother. She gets fussed when people call. She

thinks we have to have epergnes and things in aspic and fish mould when we have guests, and dessert forks."

I hadn't a clue what she was on about, but I stuck my head in and shouted, "I *love* sausages, Mrs. . . . Mrs., er?"

The house smelled of roses, sweet and warm and pink. It was like putting your head into a pomander.

"Call her Zelda," Gillian muttered.

"Zelda! Is that her name?" I thought maybe she'd made it up, the way I made up Miranda.

"Of course it's her name."

"OK," I said with a shrug, and I called out again: "I love sausages for lunch, Zelda, that'd be lovely, thank you for asking me."

There was no reply.

"She's probably wandered off someplace," Gillian explained. "She has the concentration span of a very small tadpole."

I giggled again. I am not a giggly type, as you can probably gather, but this place was making me nervous.

"Come in," she said, holding the door open wider, and I shuffled past her, curling my toes to keep the Ali Baba slippers on.

"You've got a *pink* carpet," I said, though I didn't really think this detail had escaped Gillian's attention. It's just that I couldn't *not* remark on it.

"I don't choose the color schemes," she said stiffly, in a voice that suggested she thought I probably lived under a tree root, like a Hobbit, with an earthen floor and cave paintings on the walls.

The kitchen wasn't pink. I don't suppose you can buy pink stuff for kitchens. Let's be thankful for small mercies.

"Tim said you had some good news," I said as I watched her turning the sausages under the grill.

"Yes!" she said, doing a little twirl. She had put a tea towel around her waist as an apron and she whipped it off now and flung it into the air.

"Yesssss!" she yelped again, catching the tea towel and laughing. "Wait till you hear!"

The sausages spat suddenly under the grill and a blue flame shot out with a hiss.

"The sausages are burning," I said. I wasn't trying to stop her from telling me her wonderful news, just so I could spin out the story a bit, but I didn't want the house burning down all the same.

"Blast!"

She folded the tea towel quickly to use as an oven glove and pulled the flaming grillpan out from under the grill. She set it down on the cooker top and waited for the flame to burn itself out.

"I like them charred," I said, looking at the blackened mess of sausages. It's true, I do, but I said it to be helpful.

Gillian didn't look impressed with my helpfulness. She glared at me.

"Zelda will be furious," she said. "She makes such a fuss about everything."

"Never mind," I said. "You can tell her your good news and that will take her mind off it."

"Oh no," she said. "I can't do that. I can't tell her until she's in a good mood. You never know how she might take it."

"Well," I said, "why don't we eat these and you can cook another batch for her, and she need never know."

Gillian shook her head. "She won't eat them anyway. She only eats sushi, because it's so pretty."

I gulped. I couldn't tell you whether sushi is pretty. I've never seen any. And by the way, this is not one of those books where people get anorexia. She just doesn't eat much, OK?

"Well, let's make hot dogs of them," I said, "and hide them in the bread," and I started to stuff that lovely squidgy-in-the-middle bread they had with the blackened sausages.

"Eating in the *kitchen?*" came Zelda's voice from behind me. I jumped. I hadn't heard her coming in.

I turned round and gaped at her. She looked just like her name: slim, poised, impossibly beautiful, with perfect pink-and-white skin, a tiny rosy mouth, and a pert little nose. Her auburn hair flicked itself into baby ringlets as it fell around her shoulders. She looked as if she couldn't possibly be anyone's mother. She looked about seventeen, except for her severely creased gray trousers (I bet she calls them "slacks" like my granny used to) and silver-gray polo neck and the grown-up way she wore her sleeves pushed up almost to the elbows. I couldn't imagine how this doll could be related to the—er, shall we say—less-than-elegant Gillian, with her long neck and dull little face.

"We always eat in the kitchen at home," I said, though that is not strictly true, but I thought it was best to be diplomatic.

"How quaint!" she said.

Her words seemed to ripple out of her mouth, as if she had some sort of word machine in there that just rolled them out as necessary, with no effort on her part.

"Is there any Perrier?" she asked.

Gillian put a two-liter bottle of Euroshopper water and a glass on the table.

Zelda made a face and helped herself.

"These hot dogs are delicious," I said.

"Yes," said Zelda, flashing a pink-and-white smile at me. "Thank you," she added, mysteriously.

Zelda sipped some of the water and then wafted to the kitchen door without a word. She turned at the door and smiled at us. Her smile seemed to hang in the air after she'd gone, like the Cheshire cat's.

"You see!" Gillian said.

I didn't ask what I was supposed to see; I didn't need to. I felt as if I'd eaten something very sweet and smooth and delicious but too filling, like strawberry cheesecake.

When we'd tidied up after lunch, we went upstairs to Gillian's room. It was like a hotel bedroom. It didn't look as if it belonged to anyone. There was almost nothing in it, just a bed with a yellow flowery duvet cover, a wardrobe, and a chest of drawers with a hairbrush on top and a small square mirror over it. No posters, no clothes flung about like in my room at home, no letters or concert tickets or telephone numbers tucked into picture frames—no pictures, anyway, to *have* frames—no desk, no computer, no shoes in a higgledy-piggledy line under the bed, no bookshelves, no toys left over from being younger, nothing but . . . air and furniture and a towel folded neatly on the end of the bed. Not even a calendar or a hook on the back of the door for your dressing gown. The curtains were bright, with big, splashy yellow flowers. They made me feel uneasy, though I couldn't say why, exactly.

"So what's this news, then?" I asked, though I'd lost interest at this stage. I was too busy looking around me at this peculiar house.

"The thing is," Gillian announced, throwing her arms out dramatically, "I've been invited to audition for the Yehudi Menuhin school, in England."

That was it. That was the news.

"An audition?" I said. "Like for a film?"

"No, not for a film," Gillian snapped. "I just said, for a school."

"A drama school, then? A film school?"

"No, you chump, a *music* school."

"Oh," I said. "But you'd have to go on a plane." I

suppose, looking back on it, this was not the most intelligent remark in the world, but it was the first thing that struck me. "It'd cost a fortune. And you mightn't get in after all, and then think of the waste. And anyway, what d'you want to go to school in England for? It's miles away. And it's full of English people."

She gaped at me when I said that.

"Not that there's anything wrong with English people," I said, hurriedly. I mean, I have nothing against English people, for heaven's sake, not really. All I meant was, it would be strange to be in another country, all by yourself, where everything is different. "It's just that they're . . . well, they do different stuff at school." I know this, because a friend of my father's was a teacher in England. "They do Henry the Eighth and key stages. They think the Pale is in Poland."

"I think I could manage that," Gillian said crisply. "Henry the Eighth—six wives, closed the monasteries, died a fatso. The rest I can learn. *Poland?*"

"Is it a boarding school?" I asked. I was trying to sound interested. This was obviously a big deal for Gillian, and I wasn't giving the kind of reaction she wanted.

"Of course it's a boarding school," she said. "I couldn't *commute* there, could I? It's a lovely place, out in the middle of the country. I have a brochure somewhere. An old house, like a gate-lodge, only bigger of course, with Toblerone roofs. Very pretty. And lots of music lessons."

"I'd rather have Hogwarts," I said. "Or Malory Towers."

"Well, I'm not a wizard, am I?" Gillian retorted. "Hogwarts is not on offer." She'd probably never heard of Malory Towers. You have to have a certain kind of aunt for that. "This place is very nice. I'm sure I'd like it there. It doesn't really matter what _you_'d prefer."

That stung. The air between us crackled. (It didn't actually crackle, of course. That's just a turn of phrase to indicate tension.)

"I suppose there'd be houses and all that," I said, trying to patch things over, "with competition between them? Even if it's not Hogwarts. And studies and prefects and teachers wearing funny clothes? Midnight feasts? They sound good. And cinnamon toast."

"I don't know; that's not the point," Gillian said huffily. "It's the best music school in the world. In my humble opinion. _That_'s the point. Listen, I need to practice for my audition now, so if you don't mind. . . ."

"I don't mind," I said. "May I stay and listen?"

Gillian softened a bit. That was obviously the right thing to say, but I did really want to hear, I wasn't just trying to get back into her good books. I'm not very good at getting into people's good books on purpose, if I'm honest, which. . . . Sorry, I'm repeating myself.

"OK," she said. "If you like."

I sat down on the flowery edge of the bed.

"This is a gypsy dance," Gillian said, and she tucked the violin under her chin and stuck out her bowing elbow.

She did the listening thing again, and then the music started. First, it was just this very high sort of tense music, which made you feel as if there were a teardrop inside you that was trying to fall, but couldn't. And then the music got faster and faster and it was all swirling skirts and men laughing around a campfire, the clack of heels and the flicker of knees and the dancers flashing in and out of the shadows, and it suddenly made you realize that the teardrop hadn't fallen but dissolved or turned into something else. It was like dreaming, only better.

Except that then you had to wake up. "Gill, dear," came Zelda's voice through the wall. "I'm *trying* to sleep. Could you, please . . ."

Gillian's face actually fell when her mother called out, cutting across the music. I saw it with my own eyes, or I wouldn't have believed it possible. One minute, there was Gillian's face, all high and shiny and with a sort of sparkle to it, and the next, it seemed to be about level with her chest and it had gone porridgy again.

"Sorry," Gillian called out, and lowered the violin. "You see!" she muttered to me again. "That's the reason I practice in the woods."

I felt sorry for her then. I'm a bit of a softy, deep down. I thought maybe her mother wasn't very musical.

Gillian put the violin back in its case, patting it gently

before she closed the lid, as if to apologize to it for putting it away.

"That's why she has to get away," I said darkly to Grandpa. I'd called in on him on my way home. *"Her curtains match her duvet cover.* And the walls, they're painted to match too. The exact same shade of yellow, it's . . . uncanny. Someone went to the *trouble*—"

"Yellow's cheerful," said Grandpa. "People say that."

"But it's *depressing*, everything matching like that," I said. "It's like living on one of those color cards from the people who make paint. And it's all wrong for a musician."

"What do you mean?"

"Well, how can you make proper music if you live in a place that looks like a display area in a furniture shop? It has to be bad for your soul."

"Your soul?" Grandpa said. "I didn't think you had a soul, Mags Clarke."

"That's a terrible thing to say!" I said. "Of course I have a soul. I dare say even you would discover you had a soul if you heard her play, you old codger, you."

"You think she's leaving home because of the decor?" Grandpa said. "Mags, aren't you being—"

I clapped my hands over my ears.

"Don't say it!"

"Fanciful?" my grandfather finished.

"You said it!" I said reproachfully. "I read your lips. But

you're right. It's not only that awful house. The other thing is that she wants to go to some place called the Yahooey Hooey school. They teach the violin, apparently. It's specially for 'musically gifted young people,' she says. She's dying to go there. Seems it's the coolest thing if you're into music. Only it's way off in England somewhere."

"It couldn't be called that."

"Well, something like that. She had to make a video of herself playing, and then they asked her to come for an audition."

"She must be good," said Grandpa, getting out a bottle of tonic water.

"She's fantastic," I admitted. "She can make you see things that aren't there. With your eyes shut. I hate her."

"Doesn't sound like it," said my grandfather, opening the tonic bottle with a fizzing sound.

"Well, but, she *is* super on the violin all the same," I said grudgingly. "Doesn't mean I have to love her."

"Of course not," said Grandpa. "Not in the slightest."

Tonic glugged and splashed. Ice cubes floated to the top of the glass and clinked gently against the sides in the moving tonic water.

"Oops!" I said. "Sundowner time! I'll be late, have to run. Bye, Gramps."

I dashed out, leaving the back door swinging behind me. I usually do.

Grandpa is always saying, *The day Mags Clarke closes a*

door without being specifically instructed to will be the day. . . . But
he never finishes the sentence. He can't think of a dire
enough consequence.

Next-door's baby got born and my mother went to pieces.
I had heard that your mother could go totally soppy
over a new baby, to the point where you felt completely
neglected, but I'd always thought it had to be your brother
or sister. I didn't think it could happen with a *neighbor*, especially not a new neighbor.

"It'll never fit into that cardigan," I said to Mum, looking at the little scrap as it lay on its blanket, wriggling very
slowly like an amoeba under the microscope, opening and
closing its tiny fists and yawning.

"She will," said my mother dreamily. "She'll grow into
it. You'll see."

It was a girl, evidently. I took their word for it—I certainly wasn't going to offer to change its nappy to make
sure, though my mother said there was no time like the
present for learning how to do things like that. I just gaped
at her. No way, José.

"You were that size once," my mother told me.

"So were you, I'm sure," I said. I didn't see that having
been that small once was anything to be proud of.

"Little precious," my mother crooned.

I turned a startled face to her, then realized it was the
baby who was the little precious, not me.

"So was Hitler," I added darkly.

She didn't get it. She never does.

They called her Lorna, which seems to me quite a nice name for a person, but not at all suitable for a baby. If your name is Lorna, there is no need to get insulted, because if you are old enough to read this, then you have already grown into your name, so it's all right.

One useful thing about a baby, a bit like a garden in a way, is that they are a convenient time-measurement device. You can plot your everyday life against where the baby's at now: opening its eyes, looking at you, smiling, eating off a spoon, laughing, teething, sitting up, saying "Dada." Lorna was old enough to follow your finger when you moved it in front of her eyes before I saw Gillian again.

It was in the tunnel, my own special tunnel that I had made for myself at the edge of the clearing in the woods where the stream was. It was supposed to be a secret, but I had shown it to Tim. I knew I shouldn't have, but I couldn't resist it.

It was a sort of tubular hollowing-out in the under-growth. I'd made it by wriggling in and out of the brush-wood several times with my anorak zipped up and my hood pulled down over my eyes, until the vegetation got the message and started to form itself around the shape of my burrowing body. It was like being a hare, making a form in the grass, a hidey-hole shaped to my own body, a custom-made home. It smelled of earth in there, leaves and earth and damp, and it was cold, even on warm days, because of the shade of the trees all around, and dark, but green-dark, not black-dark, a sort of leafy twilight place. Once it was made, I wasn't sure what I should do in there. There wasn't much you *could* do, except lie in it, and that got uncomfortable after a while, but I was proud of it all the same, and I went and lay in it just for the sake of it. After a while, I got to judge the proper length of time to be in there—long enough to enjoy the sensation of being enclosed, secret, hidden, and not so long that you got cramped.

I met Tim the day after I'd finished it. Some mornings, I would see that the door to the foresters' hut stood open. That usually meant he was in there, making the morning tea. There never seemed to be any other foresters about, though I could sometimes hear the whine of chainsaws in the distance, so I suppose they were off somewhere cutting trees down or planting them up or whatever they do. I think Tim was in charge of making the tea because of being the youngest, but they never seemed to come for it once he'd made it. Or maybe he took it to them and they had picnics out in the woods. When it was sunny, Tim took his chair and his mug out onto the porch, and then I could wave at him as I went by, on my way to the clearing.

This time I met him on the woodland path. He was carrying an axe or some sort of weapon like that—something to do with woodcutting—and I just blurted it out: "I've made a tunnel."

He lowered his weapon and looked down at me.

"A tunnel? You haven't been going tunneling in the woods, Mags? You can't do that, you know, it's government property."

"No, no," I reassured him. "Not a tunnel in the ground, just a sort of—oh, I suppose you could call it a den. Here, tell you what, I'll show you."

Tim wriggled his way in. His feet stuck out, and part of his legs too. I giggled at the sight of his shoes waving in the air. A space opened up between the tops of his socks and the bottoms of his trousers, revealing very white skin covered in sparse but very long brown hairs. He called out something to me, but his voice was muffled.

He worked his way out again.

"It's like a big damp lumpy duvet with stones in it in there," he said. "It's not very comfortable."

"But it's a good hiding place."

"Only for short people," he said.

"Well then," I said happily.

I didn't think to make him promise not to tell anyone. I thought he'd have known, but he's probably too old to understand that sort of thing. So that was obviously how Gillian came to hear about it.

Today (we're in the future now, I mean, the future from the point of view of the bit we've just had, but the present

from the point of view of the main part of the story; I
hope you can follow that—if you can't, you should go back
a bit and read it again, most things come clearer if you just
read the stuff carefully) I could see her shoes sticking out,
runners with mauve stripes. They looked as if Zelda might
have bought them.

"What you doin' in thar?" I called, hunkering down to
talk to her, putting on my gruffest woodland voice. It was
bad enough having this girl invading the woods with her
violin, but here—in my private place, in the tunnel I had
made myself, to fit my own body. It was too bad.

"I'm running away from home," said Gillian's muffled
voice.

"You can't be," I said, wriggling my way in past her
mauvey runners to join her. "You haven't got your under-
wear tied up in a spotted hanky like Dick Whittington
going to London."

There wasn't really enough room for two. We had to
sit—well, recline, really—very close together, so that we
could feel each other's breath on our faces. Gillian's
smelled of mustard. It made me sneeze. I managed to
catch most of it with my fingers, but some of it escaped
and made a strangled wheezing sound out of the sides of
my nostrils.

"Why are you running away?" I asked, after I'd elbowed
my way into the pocket of my jeans to get a handkerchief.

"I need to find my father," said Gillian.

"I didn't know he was lost," I said.

"Har-har," said Gillian.

"Anyway, he's definitely not in here," I added grumpily. "This is a private place."

"I'm sorry. But I couldn't think of anywhere else."

"To look for your father?"

"No, to think in."

I remembered Gillian's unspeakable mother and I felt sorry for her. Also, you certainly couldn't sit and think in that bilious yellow bedroom. You'd get heartburn.

"All right," I said forgivingly. I am actually a very kind person, in case you haven't noticed.

I lay back and looked at the leafy roof of the tunnel.

"What happened to your father?" I asked. "Are you a love child?"

Gillian giggled. "I hope so," she said, "though it's hard to imagine anyone loving my mother, isn't it?"

"That's not what a love child is," I said. "It means if your parents aren't married, or they're living together, I suppose, and you are a shameful secret."

But, of course, there's Tim, I thought. A love child is something you're only allowed one of. After that, it starts to be something you have to explain.

"I know what it means," said Gillian. "I wish I was. It sounds so romantic. Your father might turn out to be a prince, like in a story."

"Or, of course, a criminal," I said thoughtfully. "Your

father might turn out to be a criminal instead of a prince. That's more likely, really."

"What do you mean?" asked Gillian, offended.

"Considering there are more criminals than princes in the world," I explained. "Statistically, it is more likely. But how come you're looking for your father? Are you adopted?"

"No," said Gillian, wistfully. "Nothing as interesting as that."

"My father's dead," I said.

I hadn't told many people. It was hard to say, but this seemed a good moment to drop it in. I don't like telling people, but you have to mention it sooner or later, before someone says something really embarrassing.

"Oh—my—God!" said Gillian. Her hand flew to her mouth. "I'm . . . I didn't mean. . . . Oh!"

"It's all right," I said, not meaning, of course, that it was all right that he was dead, but that it was all right for Gillian to have gone on about her own father. I was glad all the same that I was lying back, staring at the top of the tunnel. It meant I didn't have to look Gillian in the eyes.

"Do you . . . ?"

"Yes," I said. "Of course I do."

"How did you know what I was going to say?"

I shrugged. What else was there to ask, except whether I missed him?

"I think we should get out," I said. "I'm starting to hyperventilate in here."

"OK," said Gillian, "only you have to go first. Last in, first out. Seeing as it's a cul-de-sac."

She pronounced the last three words in a French accent.

"*Cul-de-sac* is not the French for 'cul-de-sac,'" I said.

"Of course it is," said Gillian. She has this very adamant way of going on sometimes, just because she's older.

"No, it's not, it's 'blind alley.'"

"It can't be," said Gillian. "'Blind alley' is English."

"I mean, the French for 'blind alley' is what the French call a 'cul-de-sac,'" I said. "They never say *'cul-de-sac.'* My father told me."

That was true, but I said it to finish the argument. I knew Gillian wouldn't contradict a dead parent. Not even she would be that insensitive. I suppose I shouldn't use my dead dad like that, to score points, but you have to have *some* compensation.

I crawled backward out of the tunnel. There were bits of greenery in my hair and it felt as if there were ants running down under my collar. I scratched my scalp as I stood up.

Gillian came out bottom first. She was wearing more suitable clothes for the woods today: jeans and a long-sleeved shirt. She didn't look quite so peculiar in them. She scratched her scalp too as she stood up.

"Feels as if you're being eaten alive by very tiny creatures, doesn't it?" I said.

"Yeah," said Gillian, plonking herself on the smooth rock that I used as a table.

"Where's the violin?"

"At home."

"Why didn't you bring it?"

"I couldn't. It might have gotten damaged."

"Pity," I said. "Would you like some lunch?" I asked with sudden generosity. I am actually a very generous person, in spite of the small episode with the Kit Kat earlier, which may have given you the wrong impression.

Gillian looked at me curiously and nodded.

"It's squashed," I warned, fishing my usual tuna sandwich out of my pocket, "because of crawling into the tunnel, but it'll taste the same."

Gillian nodded again and held her hand out, palm upward, for her half of the damp sandwich.

"If we ran away from home together, they'd put us on the news, like those girls who got murdered," I said as we munched. "There'd be reconstructions with young actresses and people ringing up with false sightings. And all the time we could be in a B and B in Bundoran, watching it on the telly and eating icepops."

"That's horrible!" said Gillian.

"Yes, but we have to face these things, my mother says. She always expects me to be murdered; it's her big fear.

She has the guards' phone number written down by the phone for when it happens."

"Why does she let you out on your own, then?"

"She can't keep me locked up, can she?" I said. "I'm not allowed to talk to strangers, though."

"You talked to *me*," Gillian said.

"I don't think girls my own age count," I said.

"You talked to Tim," Gillian said. She didn't mention that she is older than me, which she is, but only by a year or two, I would say, though maybe I mentioned that already.

"Is he a murderer?" I asked.

Then old porridge-faced Gillian really surprised me. She made a joke. I didn't think she knew how.

"*Yes!*" she hissed, and made her eyes bulge. "I can't keep it a secret any longer. He's a child-murderer. Eeek! All that tree-surgeon stuff, it's just a front, just an excuse to carry chainsaws and hatchets around, but *really*. . . ."

Just for a split second there, she got me. Something icy had raced up my spine before I realized she was joking. That was the moment that I thought maybe I might get to like her after all. Possibly we might even get to be friends.

"Shu-ut up," I said with a grin. "You're not really running away, are you?"

"I was," said Gillian. "I thought I was. Sort of."

"You couldn't go without your violin."

"Oh, I wasn't going for*ever*. Just to find my dad and

then I'd go home and get the violin. I'd need it for the audition."

"Is there some connection between your father and the audition?"

"Money," she said.

"I see. Is he rich?"

"I don't know. I mean, it depends what you mean by rich, doesn't it? Not really, I wouldn't say so."

"Only, that's sort of vital information," I pointed out sensibly. I am a sensible person, in case you hadn't noticed. "There's no point in going looking for him if he isn't, is there? Since it's money you need."

"He doesn't need to be rich," Gillian said. "Just solvent."

"I thought that was something you sniffed," I said.

"It's another kind of solvent. It means not bankrupt."

Gillian was clearly pleased with herself. She'd got me back for the cul-de-sac episode. Of course, her vocabulary is not generally as extensive as mine. That was just a lucky break.

"What about your mum? Has she not got any money?"

"No. She's always moaning about it. But even if she had . . . well, you know what she's *like*."

"Well then," I said. "Come back to my house," I added on a sudden impulse.

"Why?" Gillian asked.

"We need a strategy," I said. "And a table. You always

need a table for strategic planning. To put our elbows on while we think, and to spread things out on."

"OK," Gillian said. "Lead the way."

That sounds like she thought it was a good idea, doesn't it? That's what I thought, anyway. Seems a reasonable assumption to me. But then, I'm a reasonable sort of person.

Gillian

I would like to make it quite clear that I don't usually tell people my life story, because the last thing you want is some well-meaning stranger clumping around your family, especially when things are a bit delicate, as they are in my family. So I really don't know how I got into all this playing detectives stuff. When Mags said we should try to find Dad, I sort of went along with it. To be fair, it was sort of my idea to start with. I did want to find him, because I needed to touch him for some cash, but I hadn't really thought it all through. It was only a half-formed notion that just happened to be on the top of my mind when old Mags came ambling along, and so I blurted it out, and next thing we were planning a manhunt, for all intents and purposes. As I say, I didn't really mean it to happen.

Mags

That's quite enough from her for the moment. Of course she meant it to happen. She just got cold feet later and now she's trying to justify it, that's all. You don't need to take any notice of her. I'm the one telling this story. Well then.

It was interesting doing the strategic planning, what Gillian so snootily calls "playing detectives." It was quite like being a detective, actually, only not a real one like on boring TV programs about the police where it's all Identi-Kit pictures and forensic evidence, but the kind they have in books: amateurs with inventive ways of viewing the world.

I got out the atlas and a lot of paper and pencils and a railway timetable and as many phone books as I could find and piled them all up professionally on the dining table.

"This'll do for the moment," I said. "Later, when we actually do the looking, we'll need the other sort of stuff: string, you know, and matches."

"Will we?" Gillian asked.

"Of course," I said. Clearly, Gillian hadn't read anything worth reading—always a bad sign. "Now, what's his name?"

"Brendan."

"I will need his *surname*, you eejit."

"Regan."

"OK, Brend*an* Reg*an*," I said, and wrote the name down neatly on the top line of one of the sheets of paper. "That's funny, it sort of rhymes, doesn't it?"

"How d'you mean?"

"Brendan Regan. What's he like? Is he tall and handsome and manly?" Like Tim, I was thinking. Also, since his name was practically a poem, I thought he'd have to be something special.

"Well . . . tall, yes, tall."

I wrote *tall* under the name *Brendan Regan* on my sheet of paper.

"And does he tell you wonderful stories? About the war?"

"The *war*?"

"Oh, sorry, no, that's grandfathers. Well then, about hippies."

"Hippies?"

Gillian didn't seem to know about anything that happened before about ten years ago.

"About rock 'n' roll," I explained, "and how he went to Woodstock and sat-in in the library at college and played Leonard Cohen songs on his guitar and went to

Marrakesh in the summers and campaigned to free Nelson Mandela?"

"Leonard who?"

"Gillian, what sort of a *life* did your father have? Didn't he *do* any of that cool stuff?"

"He was . . . he *is* a Web site designer," Gillian said. "He has, you know, clients? And he goes to meetings with a briefcase, and he writes down what they want and then he sends them stuff by e-mail."

"Oh. That makes him younger, I suppose."

"Than what? Younger than what?"

"Well, younger than other people's fathers. Mine, for example."

"I don't know how old he is." Really, she's hopeless, Gillian. "I never asked. It didn't seem important."

"It's not, except for the description," I explained. "When we ask the guards to help us find him, you'll need to be able to say 'midthirties' or 'late forties' or whatever, so they'll know what they're looking for."

I wrote *youngish for a dad* under *tall*.

"The *guards!*" squeaked Gillian. "We don't need to go to the police, do we?"

"Well, it depends whether we find him or not by ourselves. When did you last see him?"

"On Thursday."

"On *Thursday!*" I was taken aback, but I wrote it down dutifully all the same.

"What's wrong with that?" asked Gillian huffishly.

"I thought he was *missing*. I thought we had to *look* for him."

"He *is* missing," insisted Gillian. "I don't know where he lives. I haven't got his phone number. He's not in the phone book, by the way. I did think of that. So, I don't know how to find him. *I* call that missing."

"But he's not really missing," I said. "Not if you saw him on Thursday. I mean, he hasn't disappeared off the face of the earth or been taken hostage by terrorists or anything like that, has he?" I looked at the pile of phone books and railway timetables. Maybe I'd overdone it. "Unless he was abducted by aliens on Friday, maybe?" I added, though I didn't hold out much hope.

"There's no need to sound so disappointed," said Gillian sulkily. "I think he's living in Ballymore now. He said something about moving to be nearer to us, but I think it's because the rents are cheaper than in Dublin— that's where he was before."

"When did you have this conversation?"

Gillian thought for a moment. "About six weeks ago. Maybe two months."

"That explains why he's not in the phone book," I said. "He hasn't been there long enough. Why don't you just ask your mother how to contact him? If you saw him on Thursday, she must be in touch with him. She probably has his phone number."

"My *mother* . . . ," said Gillian. She turned her hands out, palms up and gave an exaggerated shrug. At the time, I thought she just meant, *You know how hopeless my mother is*, but now I think she meant, *Back off, don't ask too many questions.*

"OK," I said. "You don't want to involve her, right? We could just look in her address book, though, if we could find it. She has an address book, I presume?"

Gillian shrugged, so I wrote down *Zelda's address book* under the words *youngish for a dad* and then put a large black question mark after it.

Brendan Regan
tall
youngish for a dad
last seen on Thurs

Zelda's address book?

"Do you see your dad every Thursday?" I asked.

"No," said Gillian grumpily. "If I did, he wouldn't be missing, would he?"

She sounded as if she was beginning to get tired of this inquiry already. I was only getting into it.

"So, how often do you see him?"

"Every second Thursday," said Gillian. *"Not!"* she added,

when she saw the thunderous look on my face. "Not every second Thursday meaning, you know, this week and then skip a week and then next Thursday."

"I don't see what else every second Thursday could possibly mean," I said.

"I mean, the second Thursday of every month. It's sort of a standing date. We go out for a meal, usually to a steakhouse. I don't like steak. I only eat the chips. I'm thinking about becoming a vegetarian."

"Look," I said in exasperation, "can you stick to the point? We'll discuss your dietary preferences some other time. Why didn't you ask him about the money on Thursday, when you saw him?"

"I tried," Gillian said. "He didn't get it. I mean, I told him about the audition, but not about needing the money. I thought he'd see that. I didn't think I needed to spell it out. But he never offered, and then I got—well, I got too embarrassed to ask."

"You really are a complete eejit, you know that?"

Gillian suddenly thought of something. "I've got his e-mail address, if that's any use," she said. "Only I haven't got a computer."

"*I* have a computer," I said. "It was my dad's. He sort of . . . left it to me, I suppose you could say."

"You mean, I could use your computer to contact him?"

I nodded.

"Great," Gillian said. "Thanks. What'll I say?"

"How about, 'Dear Dad, I forgot to mention the other day that I need . . .' How much do you need? A hundred euro; let's say a hundred to be on the safe side. 'Dear Dad, Could you see your way to letting me have a hundred euro for my airfare to England so I can go to that audition I mentioned? Mum seems to be a bit short this week. . . .'"

"'Because you are such a mean pig,'" Gillian chimed in, "'and you always leave us short and then you come and pick me up in that stupid black car of yours and take me to that horrible restaurant where I don't even like the food, and you never want to know anything about me except what it says on my report and if I got any detentions this term, and you sigh when I mention my violin and you keep asking these questions about Zelda and whether she's *seeing* anyone, and anyway, everyone knows you love Tim more so you probably won't let me have the money and you can stuff it, I don't want it if that's your attitude.'"

Gillian banged her pink little fist down on my mother's dining table and made me jump.

"Hmm," I said, chewing on my pencil. "I don't think you should say that bit. You do want the money. What about Tim?"

"Oh, Tim hasn't got any. By the time he pays Mum for his keep and. . . ."

"No, no, I mean, does he see your dad on every second Thursday too?"

"No," said Gillian. "He won't have anything to do with him. He hates him for leaving us. For being so mean. For only seeing me once a month. For being Dad. But mostly for objecting to Tim being a forester. He wants him to be an engineer. He says being a forester is a job for a peasant."

"Oh, my!"

"Yeah. You see what we're up against. Not that Tim is a proper forester anyway, he's only doing it for the summer to see if he likes it. I don't think I can bring myself to e-mail him, the miserable swine."

"If you want the money, you'll have to."

"Don't *want* to," said Gillian, chewing her fingernails. You'd think a person who bothers with nail polish wouldn't do that.

I sighed.

"I know what," I said after a while.

"What?"

"*I'll* do it. It's my computer after all. I'll e-mail him. 'Dear Mr. Regan, You don't know me, but I am a friend of your daughter's. She desperately needs a hundred euro. If you phone her, she will explain. Her life depends on it.' No, that's too scary. 'Her future depends on it. Please get in touch. A well-wisher.'"

Gillian laughed. Her too-small face broadened and looked as if it were going to crack right across. She looked like an amused frog. She definitely didn't look like someone who'd changed her mind about looking for her father.

"I always wanted to sign something 'A well-wisher,'" I said happily. "It's so menacing."

In the end, this was the e-mail we sent:

> Dear Mr. Regan,
>
> I am a friend of Gillian's. Gillian urgently needs a cash advance for an honorable purpose. If you phone her, she will explain. I think you should get in touch. You should be very proud of your talented daughter.
>
> Yours faithfully,
>
> Margaret Rose Clarke (A well-wisher)
>
> P.S.: Gillian is a vegetarian and would like you to stop making her eat steak, as it is against her principles. She is too shy to tell you this herself. I am not shy, however, which is lucky for her. She also needs some proper clothes and a larger face.

I added the P.S. later, after Gillian had gone home, though it's not true about her being shy, or not that I'm aware of. (Have you noticed that nearly everyone in the world claims to be shy, "really"? You could try it out: ask a random group of people if they are shy "really" or "deep down inside," and you'll see what I mean. It's the same with having a sense of humor. Ask a random group of people if they have a sense of humor, and every single one of them will say that they have a great sense of humor. It's astonishing that there aren't more shy comedians in the world, to my mind.)

I took out the larger face bit before I sent the e-mail. That was only a joke between me and myself. But I left in about needing new clothes, because I thought it was true. She couldn't do something as serious as an audition in those frippy things she normally wears. The day I called at her house, she was wearing a coloredy top with a draw-string around the neck, like a laundry bag. You can't do an audition in a laundry bag.

My mother wanted to know what was going on. What were we doing, spending hours on the computer when we could be out in the sunshine?

"Oh, we go in adult chat rooms and pretend to be over eighteen," I said airily. "We thought we might find boyfriends that way. American ones."

"Mags!"

"Of course we don't," I said. "You're such a *wet*, Mum. Do you think we have no sense?"

"No," said my mother. "That is to say, yes."

"You are absolutely convinced I am going to be kid-napped and murdered and chopped up into little pieces and made into soup, aren't you?"

"Mags, don't talk like that."

"But you're wrong. I don't talk to strangers. I don't take stupid risks. I say no to drugs, though I have to admit I tried beer once at a wedding, but fortunately I didn't like it. I don't go into chat rooms. I'm all right, Mum, I'm all *right*!"

"What wedding?" said my mother. "Who gave you beer?"

"Mum, it was only a sip, but that's not the point. The point is, I'm OK."

"I suppose you are," said my mother with a small sigh.

Sometimes I wonder if she wants me to be not-OK, so she can rescue me.

"Well then," I said.

She ran her fingers absentmindedly through my hair. It was a nice feeling.

"I'm more likely to be run over by a drunk when I'm crossing at a pedestrian light," I said reassuringly, "than to be lured to my death by some weirdo with an ice-cream cone in a raincoat, I mean, in a raincoat with an ice-cream cone."

"Oh, Mags! Stoppit!" But she was grinning in spite of herself.

"Only teasing," I said.

"Emm," said my mother then, twisting a strand of my hair around her finger without realizing she was doing it. "Mags?"

"What? Leggo my hair!"

"Sorry. I . . . er, I have invited someone to lunch on Wednesday."

"Well then," I said. I wasn't terribly interested in this piece of information.

"I'd like you to be there."

"Why?" I asked suspiciously. "Why can't I just have my sandwich as usual and take it to the woods? I don't want to sit around with boring grown-ups. I'm busy next week. I'm on a manhunt."

"A *man*hunt? You're only twelve."

"It's not *that* sort of manhunt. I'm just helping someone to find someone they've . . . mislaid."

"Is that what all the e-mailing is about?"

"*One* little e-mail is all. And I didn't go online till after six, like you said, when it's cheaper."

"Hmm. Well, I'll make my famous minestrone. How does that tempt you?"

"Yum," I said. "When?"

"On Wednesday, I told you. For lunch."

"Oh! Well, all right then. I'll be there."

I may have my reservations about my mum, but I know good minestrone when I get it. I believe in being fair about things and I cannot say fairer than this: if you haven't tasted my mother's famous minestrone, you really haven't tasted minestrone at all. (Except possibly in Sicily.)

Gillian's father did not reply to my e-mail. I was furious. Surely to goodness any father worth the name would reply to a mail like that from his own daughter. Practically from his own daughter.

I tried to imagine what my dad would have done if someone had e-mailed him like that, but I couldn't decide how he would have reacted. I just had no idea how he would behave. That made me feel a bit panicky, as if the earth were shifting under my feet and I didn't know which way to jump to safety.

Sometimes, his face won't come into my head and I can't imagine him anymore. That makes me feel panicky too, and guilty as well. It's as if I am losing him all over again, only this time, it's my fault. When I feel like that, I go and look at the photos in the album we keep in the side-board. I stare at the photographs for a while, looking at his face smiling over the top of a book or peeping out from behind a gate—the back gate of our old house, the one that led into the lane where the woodbine grew—and finally something in my memory slides and clicks into place, and the smiling photo face starts to move and talk and gradually my own remembered image of my dad's face comes swimming back into my mind and takes over from the photograph, and it's almost like remembering him properly. Only not really.

Sometimes, when the panicky feelings started, I would screw up my eyes and try to squeeze a few tears out. I had an idea that a good cry would flush the feelings away. That's what people say. But my eyes just got hot and dry and the tears wouldn't come. I'd have to think about all the sad things about him being dead before I could manage even a sniffle.

I'd think about how I was an orphan now, or half an

orphan. That was no good, because it only made me laugh, imagining myself cut in half, hopping about on one leg. Laughter is good, but there are times when it is *not* appropriate.

I'd think about how Mum had no one to talk to about things, no one to plan things with, no one to share the responsibility of a child with. Of course, I am a very easy child to bring up, but all the same, it is a big responsibility to be a parent all by yourself. That just makes me sigh with frustration and check guiltily that my mobile is charged up. It's difficult to feel sad about my mother's parenting problems. I mean, I understand it's hard for her, but it doesn't push the sadness buttons, you know?

I'd think about how we'd had to sell our old beloved creaky house in the city and come and live in this stupid house where everything is too new and shiny and there is too much light everywhere and no nooks and crannies. But even that didn't make me cry. The new house is annoying, not sad; leaving the old house was sad, but not as sad as losing Dad, so there's no point in whining about it.

I would think about the terrible noise there'd been when he'd collapsed onto the horn of the car, and how my mother and I had come running out of the house, thinking someone was trying to steal it, and how we'd found him slumped there, not breathing, and the horn blaring and blaring like some angry creature. That makes me edgy and nervous, though, not sad exactly.

I'd think about how much I missed him. I'd think about how he used to tease my mother when she got anxious about things, stood up for me when my mother was being strict. I'd think about how he used to let me beat him at chess and how he used to read to me when I was younger and about how, when I got older, I used to read to him when he was too tired to read for himself after a long day's work and how we used to laugh about things that happened in books. That makes me sad, sad, in a longing, aching sort of way.

But the very saddest thing I didn't want to think about.

Gillian

I wasn't the slightest bit surprised to hear that my father hadn't replied to the e-mail. Really, Mags is too ridiculous. What does she think? That she can *make* people nice by sending them cute little notes, inviting them to join the human race? It doesn't work like that. She doesn't understand that yet. She hasn't had the experience, I suppose, of having her dad go missing on purpose. I know it's terrible if someone dies, because you know you will never, ever see them again, but if someone just walks away from you, *chooses* to walk away, that's much worse, because it spoils everything. Not just everything now and in the future, but the past as well. All those games he played with you when you were a kid, all the stories you read together, all the walks you had, the bags of toffees he brought home on a Saturday—they're all tainted now, as if someone has spat on your memories, because the person you shared them with turns out not to have loved you after all. OK, maybe he loved you at the time, but he didn't love you enough to stick it out. That's what makes it so bad.

I suppose I should try to see it from Mags's point of

view. She would probably give anything to see her dad again, just once, and that probably makes her think that for me, seeing my dad even once a month is like being given the most wonderful birthday present. But he's still missing, my dad, that's what she doesn't understand. Being missing doesn't have to do with whether you've seen a person recently. Being missing has to do with whether you know where to find them if you need them. It's easy to turn up once a month, all smiles and with the welcome of the world for yourself. That's not the same as being *available*, which is what parents are *supposed* to be.

And now, I am supposed to write to the school and say whether I am coming to the audition, by Wednesday of next week.

"Better tell them you're coming anyway," was Mags's insightful advice.

"I couldn't do that," I said. "It mightn't be true." I don't like to tell lies. It makes me uncomfortable.

"Well then," she said, "tell them you 'would be happy to accept'. That's true, you *would* be happy to accept, even if you can't."

I suppose I'll have to do something like that, to keep my options open. I wish I didn't have to *deal* with all this. I wish I could just concentrate on the music. That's what's important to me, not all this stuff with letters and e-mails and is this a lie and is that the truth and what will it cost and where the blazes is Dad when you need him? The music is the thing. It's hard to explain to someone on the outside, but going into the music is like going to another place, where everything is different. Not always better, but different, because the rules are different.

When I'm nervous or agitated, I pick up my violin for comfort, just like the way I used to hug my teddy when I was a little girl.

"Did you have a teddy when you were little?" I asked Mags.

She frowned at me.

"Listen," I said, and I started to play "The Teddy Bears' Picnic."

She frowned harder. "That's so familiar," she said. "What is it?"

"If *you* go down to the woods today . . . ," I sang softly, "dee-doodly, dee-doo, dee-*doo*."

Mags grinned and started to pick up the tune. "Dee-doo, dee-doo, dee-diddly-dee-die," we sang together, "dee-diddly-dee-die, dee-diddly-dee-die. . . ."

"Today is the day the teddy bears have their *pic* . . . nic!" Mags sang. "I haven't heard that since I was about five!"

Then I held the bow straight up in the air and used my fingers to pick at the strings. *Ooh-ooh-ooh, eeh-ooh, eeh-ooh,* went the violin.

"*Pizzicato,*" I said over the sound, in answer to Mags's puzzled look. "It's allowed." Honestly, she knows nothing.

She laughed. "Sounds like something you get in an Italian restaurant. Pizzicato with mushrooms."

"Comfort food," I said.

Mags

It came to me in the middle of the night. That probably means I am some sort of genius; the sort of person who is struck by inspiration at the midnight hour. I try not to let the idea go to my head, but it is interesting to think about it all the same. People probably think Gillian is the genius around here, just because she can play the fiddle. They don't know about my inspirations, or they might think differently. It's just that some talents are more hidden than others. Some people are not such show-offs that they have to go wafting about the *forest* with a musical instrument.

My mum doesn't sleep well. She says she still hasn't gotten used to sleeping by herself, and I often hear her creeping around making tea in the kitchen in the dead of night. Then I lie there feeling bad about her not sleeping. Or not so much about my mum not sleeping, but about what a useless daughter I am. I can't bring myself to get up and go and say something comforting to her, the way a really good daughter would do. Or even just sit with her and say nothing. I really wish my mum and I got on better. We don't fight, it isn't that, but there is always this stiffness between us. I can't remember when it started.

I wondered what Gillian would do. I couldn't imagine anyone sitting with Zelda in the night, but Gillian might sit with my mum, if she were *her* mum. At this point my thoughts became confused and I drifted into sleep. I didn't hear my mother's door shutting softly as she went back to bed.

Later, though, I woke again and shot up in bed, slapping myself across the mouth to stop myself shouting out. This was the moment of inspiration, the one I just told you about if you were paying attention.

That's why! was what I had to stop myself shouting. It had come to me in a dream, I thought, or else just as I woke up. I knew, suddenly, what my dad would do if he got an e-mail from a friend of his daughter's that he had never heard of. I had no idea why I hadn't been able to imagine it during the daytime, since it was so obvious.

"Who the blazes is *that?*" he'd have muttered irritably. "Macla, what sort of a name is that?"

Macla is my e-mail username. In case you can't work it out for yourself, I will explain that it is made up from the first few letters of my real name and surname. It's cool, isn't it? Like a Celtic goddess, or a saint who was dead holy and built a lot of monasteries and led an army to defeat the heathen. Of course, my father knew what my e-mail name was, but *Gillian's* dad obviously wouldn't know that. It was Gillian's dad who would scrunch over his computer screen and mutter about the unknown Macla.

I snuggled down again under the duvet with a smile,

pleased as punch with myself that I'd worked it out. I hadn't forgotten my dad after all.

As I drifted toward sleep, I remembered what Gillian had said about having a teddy. I did have a teddy: Teddy Murphy he was called, after a cat we used to have, only the cat was called Murphy, not Teddy Murphy, obviously. I hadn't seen the old fellow since the move. I'm too big for a teddy, of course, but still, I'd like to know where he is. I'd like to be able to put him on a shelf in my bedroom, just for decoration, and look at him sometimes. I wouldn't like to think of him being squashed in the bottom of a leftover tea chest or with his coat all dusty in the garden shed.

Gillian

She really has no sense, Mags. I suppose I have to make allowances for her age. But she comes out with things all jumbled up, and it can be very confusing. I didn't mean to go stomping all over her feelings in my size 12s, but how was I to know what she was on about? (She doesn't really wear size 12 shoes, by the way, but this is just the kind of very obvious figure of speech Gillian uses. To be quite fair, since we're on the subject, her feet are not her worst point. I'd say they're about a size 5, if you want to know. Signed: *Mags*)

"My dad got a virus," she said excitedly to me a couple of days after we'd sent the e-mail, when we met in this place she calls her den. It's just a clearing by the stream in the woods, with a sort of hidey-hole beside it. Very childish.

I was just opening up my lunch: peanut-butter sandwiches, because I was experimenting with vegetarianism.

"About a year and a half ago," she was burbling on.

"What sort of virus?" I asked. I know you shouldn't ask questions about other people's illnesses, but for goodness' sake, she was volunteering this information; she obviously needed to tell me. The least I could do was show a bit of interest.

"Oh, I don't know." She shook her hair in that impatient way she has. "That's not the point."

"I'm sorry," I said. "I didn't mean to intrude. You don't have to tell me about it, if it's private." I think that was fair enough. I wasn't going to poke my nose into her family's business, even if she insisted on taking a magnifying glass to mine.

"It's not private," she said. "It was one of the ones you get by e-mail."

"E-mail!" My God, I thought, she is all over the place, this child. "You can't die of an e-mail virus!"

OK, OK, I made a mistake, but I ask you, what would you think if someone's dad has died, and suddenly she starts going on about him getting a virus?

"I know that," she said, looking all mystified. "What are you talking about? Oh! You think I meant . . . Oh, Gillian! He didn't catch that kind of virus. I mean he got a virus on his *computer*."

"Oh," I said. "Sorry."

Well, so I got red in the face. So I'm a sensitive soul. Artists are like that.

"I remembered it in the night," Mags went on, galloping off somewhere else now. I told you, she's all over the place. "The thing is, see, it took him ages to get rid of it, the virus, and ever after, he was very picky about e-mails from strangers. He never opened anything unless he knew the person, and even then, only if there was no attachment. He was always warbling on about it. And *your* dad works with computers, right, so he's probably very careful too, which explains why he hasn't answered my e-mail. He probably put it straight in the bin. That *explains* it!"

"Could be," I said, careful not to sound too convinced. You don't want to be encouraging a person with this sort of wild imagination. "Yeah, I s'pose. Or it could just be that he doesn't care. Mentioning money mightn't have been the best thing. If we'd just said he should ring me. . . ."

"But listen," Mags said. She interrupts. She's always doing it. "The other thing I thought of in the night is this: why don't we text him? I'm sure he has a mobile."

"I told you, I don't have his phone number." I was beginning to get a bit weary of this whole hunt-the-dad game, and she wasn't even very good at it, as far as I could see. "If we had that, we could just have rung him in the first place." That was a no-brainer, I would have thought.

"No, I know that, but what about your mum? Has *she* got a mobile? Because if *he* has a mobile, and *she* has a mobile. . . ."

"Oh, bling-bling!" I said. "They can ring each other up and have nice little chats. What use is that?"

"Because, stupid," said Mags with her usual tact and charm, "it means she probably has his number programmed into *her* mobile."

I don't take kindly to being called stupid, but I let it go, because actually, she was beginning to make a bit of sense after all. It might be worth a try, I thought.

"Mmm," I said. I didn't want to sound too excited, in case she got carried away again. "Yeah, she has a mobile. She lends it to me if I have to go somewhere, because I haven't got one."

"There you go. Perfect. You can invent a trip somewhere, borrow her mobile, and Bob's your uncle."

Mags was so pleased with herself, she did a little twirl and took a bow. "Who's a clever girl, then?" she asked triumphantly.

I thought it best to humor her, so I grinned halfheartedly.

"It was a brain hemorrhage, if you must know, not a virus," she said suddenly, sitting down with a bump. "That my dad died of. He just collapsed one day, sitting at the wheel of his car outside the house, and fell over onto the horn. It made a terrible racket, and that was that. Out on a blast."

Well, what a thing to land on me out of nowhere! I didn't know where to look. I don't know what I said. I suppose I said something like, "Oh dear, I mean, I'm sorry." Something sympathetic, I suppose. I hope. I wouldn't like to think I said anything offhand, though I was in such a state of surprise, I probably wasn't exactly as warm and sensitive as I would have been if I'd had time to think about it.

"Well then," she said, which she always does when she doesn't know what to say, and she shrugged.

Mags

Of course it was an absolutely brill idea. She just can't bear to admit it.

Our first go at texting Gillian's dad, when we eventually got ahold of her mother's mobile, went like this:

pls ring Gill. she nds help.

"Sounds as if I'm suicidal," said Gillian. "Or an alcoholic."

"OK," I said brightly, and changed the text so that it read:

pls ring gill. she nds money.

"It doesn't sound very enticing, does it?" said Gillian.

"Enticing? You want enticing?" I said. "OK, you've got enticing." And I jabbed at the phone with my thumbs and came up with this:

pls ring gill urgently

"That'll scare him," said Gillian.

I should have sensed that her heart wasn't in it.

"Good," I said. "Serve him right for not answering our e-mail. Will I send it?"

Gillian looked carefully around, as if she were afraid someone might see us doing something terrible, and said, "OK, send it."

I jabbed again at the phone and then I said, "Right, done. That should shift him."

We sat for a few moments staring at the phone, expecting it to burst into a frenzied peeping at any moment.

"We said to ring *you*," I said at last. "So he probably won't text back on your mother's phone. He'll call you at home, when he gets a chance."

"Yeah," said Gillian. "Sure."

But he didn't call her at home that day. Or the next.

"Well, text him again," I said impatiently when Gillian reported this sorry news. "Same message, only this time, type *URGENTLY* in capital letters."

"It won't work," said Gillian glumly. "I know he won't ring. He doesn't care. I won't get the money, and I won't be able to go and I'll miss the audition, and I'll blow my one chance, and I'll never get to be a professional violinist, and I'll end up working in a supermarket and it'll be all his fault."

"Sounds as if that's what you *want* to happen," I said. "You're giving up awfully easily. Anyway, a supermarket could be quite good. You'd probably get free sweets."

I was only trying to look on the bright side, but Gillian glared at me. It seemed to me she was sort of pleased that her dad was being so difficult to track down. I thought maybe she needed an excuse not to do the audition after all. Perhaps she was scared.

"Well, I'll send the text again, but I can't see it having any more effect than the first one," she said stubbornly.

"But there must be tons of other things you could do," I said, "even if we don't find your dad. You could tell your mother. I know you don't want to, but she is your mother after all, she'd be bound to help if she knew how much you want to do this. Or you could get Tim in on it. Or you could borrow the money somewhere."

"A hundred euro? Who do you know who would lend a thirteen-year-old a hundred euro?"

"Well, you could borrow twenty from one person," I said, "and twenty from another, build it up that way. I could lend you twenty-seven euro thirty; I have twenty-five in my post office book and I have two thirty in my pocket." Have I pointed out before that I am a generous soul? Well, in case you haven't noticed, that was quite a big offer, not so much the money in the post office—you don't notice if you give that away—but offering her the two thirty in my pocket was quite a big deal, I thought. But she didn't seem to notice. "Tim could probably lend you twenty or thirty," I went on. "My mum might lend you twenty if we asked her nicely. That's more than half of a hundred already. My grandpa . . . well, he's pretty poor, but he might rise to ten. Be creative! Haven't you got a godmother or someone? Do you not get money for your birthday sometimes? Have you got a post office book of your own? Can you sell something? There are a thousand things you could do, I'm sure there are."

I wanted to shake Gillian. Where's her imagination? Hello?

"I couldn't pay people back, though," she pointed out obstinately. Did she really want to go to this audition or not?

"Gillian, you keep putting obstacles in the way. Think positive! If you start doing other things to raise the money, you'll find he'll probably ring. Things always work that way."

"No, they don't," Gillian muttered. "I hate my life."

Sometimes I think maybe she's a bit spoiled.

Gillian

I was starting to regret having told Mags I wanted to find Dad. I mean, it *would* have been very handy if I knew where he was. I could just go and talk to him and ask him for the money, and he could say yes or no. Probably no, but at least then I'd know where I stood. But I was starting to feel a bit uneasy about all this tracking down. I figured, if he doesn't want me to know where he lives, that means he doesn't want me to come bothering him. And really, I can't allow myself to be distracted by all this stuff. I need to be putting my energy into my music. I do not need to be having woodland adventures and playing at manhunts, however amusing Mags finds it. It seems to me that Mags is more interested in the idea of finding my dad than in the idea of making it possible for me to go to my audition.

Still, I did as she suggested and sent the second text message.

Result: nothing.

Precisely as predicted.

Mags

That is so unfair! Don't listen to her! It wasn't for my amusement, all this. What do I care about Gillian's father? As far as I am concerned, he is a cipher. (By the way, this is one of those words you might think you understand, but you probably don't, even if you can use it properly. Isn't that amazing? To think that you can totally misunderstand a word and still be able to use it correctly!) His role, in my view, was simply to supply the cash Gillian needed to go to England to do her audition. Period.

Anyway, I had other things on my mind for a while. Things closer to home.

I found a dress I'd forgotten I owned, a sleeveless cotton summery thing with tiny flowers on it. It was creased from being folded up, but I shook it out and hung it in the bathroom while I had a shower, and it looked better after that. I sniffed it carefully. It smelled a bit musty, but not actually stinky. I sprayed it with hair stuff I found in the bathroom cabinet to freshen it up. Then it smelled sweet but still musty and the fabric had gone stiff in places. Still, it wasn't too noticeable. I dried myself off and put on the dress and looked at myself in the mirror. It was a little tight, but not very uncomfortable. It'd be OK.

I blow-dried my hair. I never do that normally, I just brush it swiftly and let it dry naturally, hanging about my shoulders. The blow-drying made it go all wispy. I hoped I didn't look a complete dork. I pulled it back and put a hairslide at the back of my head, in that old-fashioned style my mother likes, the way Victorian girls used to wear their hair. I wished I could get those cool tiny braids in it. A girl at my last school got those done in a hotel in Lanzarote and she didn't have to so much as touch it for more than six weeks. That's my idea of a really useful hairstyle. I didn't think my mother would take me to Lanzarote specially, though. An alternative would be to have it cut really short, but my mother doesn't like that idea. She's romantic about long hair.

The way I'd pulled my hair back made my face seem extra wide. I pulled at the front a bit, to loosen it from the slide, and get some of it to loop artistically down by my forehead. It didn't look too bad. I brushed my teeth and put on a bit of lip stuff, the kind you use to keep away chapped lips in the winter. It tasted of strawberries.

"You'll do," I told the mirror grimly, and launched myself off up the corridor toward the kitchen.

My mother was stirring a large pot and sniffing the juicy steam that came off it when I put in an appearance. She's not the world's greatest cook, but she is great at soup and stew.

"Delicious!" I pronounced, sniffing the rich, tomatoey air.

"My goodness!" said Mum. "You scrub up well. Must buy you a new summer dress, though. You look like you are going to burst forth at any moment from that one. Can you breathe?"

"Are you calling me fat?" I asked suspiciously.

"I'm calling you a growing girl, is all," said my mother.

"I *knew* I should have worn jeans," I said sulkily. "I feel a twit in this. I'll change. I have a clean blouse somewhere."

"No, don't. You're lovely. My lovely daughter!"

I grimaced. I wasn't used to compliments and I didn't know what to do when they came.

"So who's coming to lunch, anyway?" I asked, peeking through the door to the dining room. There was a check tablecloth and a tiny vase of delicate flowers in the middle of the table and cutlery for three. "That Miss What's-her-face from the library? Or Grandpa?"

I didn't really think it was likely to be Grandpa. He doesn't like my mother's cooking. "Too wet," he'd said once, when I asked him what was wrong with it. He liked a nice dry piece of meat that you could see, three potatoes, and a boiled vegetable, preferably green. "That you could see" meant no gravy or sauces smothering the meat, and nothing chopped up and mixed with other stuff. Still, he made an exception for her minestrone. Her minestrone was exceptional.

"His name is Don," my mother said, far too casually.

"A *man!*" I gasped.

If my mother had invited a discombobulated llama or a number 59 bus to lunch I couldn't have been more surprised.

"Indeed," said my mother drily. "Most people of that name tend to be male, and this one is certainly old enough to be beyond calling a boy."

"You're being smart," I said accusingly. "You're never smart. What's wrong?"

"Nothing is wrong, Margaret Rose. I am merely inviting someone to lunch."

"Is he your boyfriend?"

"No!"

"Do you wish he was your boyfriend?"

"Mags! I hope you won't talk like that when Don is here. If you're going to embarrass me. . . ."

"I don't see how you could have met someone to fall in love with already," I said. "We've only been here a month."

"I am *not* in love with him. And I didn't meet him since we moved here. I've known him all my life. He's an old friend, of mine and your dad's. He's in the area, passing through, so I invited him. Now will you stop going on about him like that? You're making me nervous."

"Sweet peas on the table," I said. "Hmm."

"It's July. We often have sweet peas on the table in July."

"Was he your boyfriend before Daddy was?"

"Mags, I'm warning you. . . ."

"OK, OK," I said with a sigh.

Don turned out to be quite nice. Boring but nice, the way grown-ups often are. He asked me what class I was in at school. I explained that it was the summer holidays and I wasn't at school. My mother kicked me under the table.

"I have just finished at primary school," I went on sweetly, "so I'm starting secondary in September, in the next village. It's just a few miles away."

"Town," my mother said. "If you call Ballymore a village, you won't be very popular around here. You aren't even allowed to call Ballybeg a village, and goodness knows. . . ."

Ballybeg is the place we live on the outskirts of ("Of which we live on the outskirts" is more correct, but I thought you might find it hard to get your head around that.).

"Ally*beg* is definitely a village," I said to Don. "Two streets and a SuperValu. And twenty-five pubs, of course."

"Seven," said my mother, "one of which is really more a restaurant, and a new housing estate over beyond the woods, and a bus stop."

"So you can get out of it," I murmured.

"But Ballymore is positively sophisticated by comparison," my mum went on. "It has an *arts* center, Don, and two gasoline stations, and there's a patisserie opening in the autumn. Plus a primary school *and* a secondary."

"As you see," I said to Don, "I was wrong. It's clearly a town, Ballymore. Practically a city. The patisserie pushes it up a class, I'd say."

Don smiled. He looked too old to be anyone's boyfriend, but even so, I thought I'd better make quite sure.

"Did you know my dad in the olden days?" I asked.

"We were in college together," said Don. "All three of us. He and I and your mother." He put on a solemn face. "I was very shocked to hear of his death. I'm sure you miss him terribly."

"We do," I said. "Especially Mum. It's very sad for her. She's desperate for a new baby."

Don looked embarrassed. "Oh dear," he murmured, and dabbed his mouth with his napkin.

"Mags!" said my mum loudly. "That's not true. And even if it were. . . ."

"Well, you went totally soppy over Lorna," I retorted. "That's next-door's baby," I explained to Don.

"I didn't. She's a lovely baby, I like babies. It doesn't mean . . . what you said."

I looked at Don and shrugged. "Sorry. I take it back," I said. "She's perfectly normal, really. I didn't mean she'd be the type to steal babies out of their prams outside supermarkets."

"Mags!"

"*Now* what have I said?"

"Get the dessert, please," said my mother weakly.

"And then may I go? I have an important meeting."

Don tittered.

"Do you think children can't have important meetings?" I challenged him when I came back into the dining room, carefully carrying a plate with a magnificent summer pudding on it, leaking delicious-looking purple juices. I adore summer pudding. If your parents don't know how to make it, I suggest you find a cookbook with a recipe for this fabulous dessert in it and give it to them for Christmas. I wouldn't recommend you learn to make it yourself, because once you start on that, you are on a slippery slope that ends with you taking out the dustbins and scrubbing the kitchen floor.

"Oh, I'm sure they can," he blustered; Don, I mean. "I'm sure they can."

"My friend has been called to an audition for the Yahooey-Manooey school," I went on haughtily. "She needs some assistance with her plans."

"The Yehudi *Menuhin* school? My goodness, that *is* important."

"You've heard of it?" I was surprised. I'd been half thinking Gillian might have made up the whole thing. I'm not calling her a liar, more a fantasist.

"It's world-famous. Your friend must be a star musician."

"She's fabulous," I said proudly. "She can really make that fiddle sing."

"I thought she wasn't your friend," my mother intervened. "I thought you didn't even like her."

"She takes getting to know. She's a bit off-putting at first. Terribly serious. And her face is too small."

"Ah yes," said Don, "talented people can be rather distant."

"Exactly," I said gravely. "And they expect you always to play second fiddle to them. They seem to think other people are only sausage-eaters."

"Nothing wrong with eating sausages," said Don stoutly.

I cheered up at that. Maybe he wasn't so bad. He's obviously a big summer pudding fan too, so he must have his priorities right.

"And besides," Don said, "even the most talented performers in the world are nothing without an audience. Have you ever thought of it that way? Somebody has to appreciate their performance, or it's wasted. They might as well grow potatoes or whittle sticks if nobody cares to listen."

"Well then," I said.

I hadn't thought of it that way, as it happens, but he is so right, when you think about it. He's a remarkably intelligent fellow, really, all told.

Gillian

I couldn't believe it when Mags told me what she'd said to her mother's friend. She gets away with it because she's such a child, I suppose.

"You *didn't*!" I squealed. "Why did you say that about your mother?"

Did I mention before about Mags's deficiencies in the tact and diplomacy department? Possibly not. But believe me, she could learn a thing or two from a crab about keeping your mouth shut and your eyes open.

"To warn him off, of course," she said, tossing her hair, only with that new hairstyle, it doesn't work so well. "Men are always terrified of women who want babies. And anyway, it's true."

What does she know about what men are afraid of? She's only eleven. (Oooh, that's so not true! I'm twelve and a quarter. She's always trying to make me sound much younger than her. It's just so she can boss me around. Signed: *Mags*)

"But why would you want to warn him off?" I asked. "Why shouldn't your mother have a boyfriend if she wants one?"

I wish someone would be *my* mum's boyfriend. Then we might start to have something like a life in our family.

"I would have thought that was obvious," Mags said pompously. She can be quite a pompous little madam when she wants.

"It's not obvious at all," was all I said. I didn't want to provoke her.

"But my dad. . . ."

"Is dead," I said flatly.

I didn't mean it to come out rudely. I just meant to shake her out of her haughty mood, but as soon as I'd said it, I realized I'd gone too far. You have to be careful around people who have had a death in the family. They're sort of fragile and spiky at the same time.

There was a moment of complete silence between us. The stream gurgled complacently on.

"Well," Mags said stiffly, at last, "I suppose I shouldn't have expected much sympathy from *you*, with your violin and your snooty mother and your wandering father and your precious audition."

I gasped. Now she was the one who was going too far.

"I thought you were on my side," I said.

"And I thought you were on mine."

We glowered at each other, our elbows on the flat rock she claims is a table, our chins resting on our hands. The silence between us stiffened. You could almost taste the anger in the air. She was plainly the one in the wrong. OK, I'd been a bit insensitive, but she was the one who'd attacked me and my family. But I'm older, so I thought the best thing was to resist the impulse to snarl at her.

"Your dress is pretty," I said at last, for something friendly to say.

"It doesn't fit," she said, but she looked as if she might be thawing out a bit. There was silence again for a while, but it was a slightly friendlier silence. "Sorry," she added eventually.

"Yeah, same here," I muttered. "Sorry."

I didn't mind apologizing, once she said it first. She was the one who'd insulted me, after all.

Then she changed the subject. She asked me if I'd told the people at the school that I was coming for the audition.

"Today's the deadline," she said, as if I didn't know.

I had accepted, of course.

"It's in two weeks," I said, "and I still don't see how I'm going to get there."

"We'll think of something," she said. Alarm bells started to ring for me. She was off on her quest again. "We'll just have to fall back on our own resources, is all. There are lots of things we can try."

"But I have *so* much practice to do," I wailed. "I should be working six or seven hours a day, and all I do is sit around sending text messages and working out ways to contact Dad."

"Six or seven hours!" she gasped in amazement. "That's torture!" You see what I mean. People just don't understand.

"No, it isn't," I said. "It's what you do if you are a real musician. I do three, sometimes four. But it's not enough before an audition."

"OK," said Mags. "Tell you what. You concentrate on your practicing, I'll do the rest."

I shook my head, but what could I say? I couldn't very well stop her, and besides, it would be useful if she found him for me and delivered him like a trout in a net. A trout with a check for a hundred euro in its mouth!

"I have an idea," she said.

I don't like Mags's ideas. They are all half-baked and come out of books, as far as I can tell. She thinks she's Hercule Poirot or the Secret Seven or someone.

Mags

"Brendan Regan?" said Grandpa, leaning back in his armchair and giving his toes a delighted wiggle. He loves to be consulted. "Of course I know him. Obviously, I know the locals—I've lived here all my life. The Regans, now let me see. Yes, they used to live a mile or two out the road, they had a dairy farm, but after the old man died— terrible farmer he was—they sold up and moved into town, into that new estate over the other side of the woods. Brendan was never interested in farming. Just as well, if he was going to turn out as bad a farmer as his father. He's in computers, something like that. He has his own business, very successful I believe. Drives a flash car. Married a foreigner, I think. Or maybe she's from Dublin. What do you want to know for?"

I hugged myself. "Oh, just making inquiries," I said.

My grandfather laughed. "You're up to something, aren't you?"

"I wouldn't say that," I said mysteriously. "Is he separated?"

"From his wife? Hmm, I heard that, yes. She's peculiar, I believe. An opera singer, if you don't mind."

"Really?" I said, remembering Zelda's beautiful speaking voice. An opera singer was certainly a bit unusual in Ballybeg, but even if she'd been a bank clerk, people would have called Zelda peculiar. "And where does he live now?"

"How should I know?" Grandpa was turning grumpy again. He only liked questions that he knew the answers to.

I thought carefully before my next move. There was no point in saying anything that would make Grandpa even grumpier. The thing was not to make him uncomfortable by asking a question he couldn't answer.

"I bet you could find out, though," I said at last. "I'm sure you have contacts. You know everything that happens around here, I'd say."

"Oh, I could find out if I really wanted to know," he agreed.

I said no more. No point in pushing my luck. I'd wait and see.

Grandpa came up with the goods, as I had known he would. It was two days later. I was making a jam sandwich in his kitchen. Grandpa always has a good range of jams to choose from. Raspberry today, I thought, though I don't like the tiny raspberry pips. They stick in your teeth. Someone told me once that the jam people had the pips made specially out of wood to put in the jam, so people would think it was really made of raspberries, but I didn't believe that. It was obviously made of raspberries, because it tasted of raspberries. Besides, there was a picture of raspberries on the front of the jar. That clinched it, in my view.

The door creaked open. I wasn't surprised. My grandfather always opens doors by pushing at them with his stick. I knew he'd shuffle in after the door in a moment, and he did.

"That Brendan Regan you were asking about," he said.

"Hmm?" I said, not looking at him, pretending not to be all that interested. I carefully lined up the top slice over the bottom slice and reached for a bread knife.

"He's living over in Ballymore, on the main street, in a flat over the dry cleaner's."

"Is he?"

"He is. Why do you want to know?"

"Oh, it's just that . . . Hey! There's a wasp! They love jam, don't they? Bit early, though, for wasps, isn't it?"

There was no wasp. I just didn't want to have to answer my grandfather's awkward questions, so I went hunting around the kitchen with a rolled-up newspaper and whooshed the imaginary wasp out the window.

Gillian

"Over the dry cleaner's!" I said. My nose curled up when Mags told me what she'd found out. "It must be smelly!"

"Yes," she said. "But that's not important. The point is, we know where to find him. Will we pay him a little visit?"

I didn't answer. Mags looked up from the hole she'd been digging with a dessert spoon by the side of the "table" rock. She was hollowing out a shallow depression in its shade. It would be a good place to keep her lunch, she'd said, in the cool of the rock's shadow, and with the bottom of the lunch box nestled into the damp earth. Not that she owned a lunch box, but I suppose she could acquire one, now that she was going to have a woodland larder to keep it in. Quite the little Maid Marian, she is.

"We could go tomorrow," she said after a few moments.

Tomorrow! Well, there was no point in postponing it indefinitely, I suppose, and I did still need the money.

"I suppose so," I said.

"I thought you'd be pleased!" she said, and gave another ferocious dig with her spoon. "Do you not *want* to see him?"

"I do, yeah," I said, though I didn't exactly want to see *him*. I wanted to get the money so I could go to the audition. Mags didn't seem to get that. I think she thought this was all about bringing father and daughter together. Some hope of that!

"OK," she said. "Meet you here tomorrow, ten o'clock?"

"No, I told you," I said, though actually I don't think I had, "I practice in the mornings."

"All right, at lunchtime so." She's a persistent little pest.

I didn't answer.

"Well then," Mags said, "after lunch. Say three o'clock? I think the afternoon bus is at three-thirty. I'll check."

I nodded.

"Durn newsince," I heard her muttering under her breath in that stupid voice she puts on sometimes. I hope *I* wasn't the nuisance. Cheeky monkey!

Mags

Gillian didn't turn up the next day. I waited fairly patiently till ten past, then a quarter past three. I started to get jumpy after that. If Gillian didn't come soon, we'd miss the bus. I'd give her five more minutes.

I sighed and rested my elbows on the table rock. It hadn't rained for ages and the stream was low. It trickled over its stony bed and chattered quietly to itself. You'd never think it was the same stream that usually whisked busily down from the hills, rabbiting on to itself at nineteen to the dozen, no time to stop and chat. I felt a bit like the lazy stream today, not much whiz and bounce. It had gotten terribly hot. I suppose that was why.

Three twenty-one. Still no sign of Gillian. Maybe she'd got delayed. In that case, there would be no point in her coming to meet me here. If she had any sense, I thought, she would have decided to go straight to the bus stop, hoping I would think to meet her there instead. Yes, that's probably what had happened, I told myself. I checked my watch again. Still three twenty-one. If I raced, I might make it. I'd forgotten to check the timetable, but I was pretty sure the bus went at three thirty or thereabouts.

I was sorry now that I was wearing my going-visiting clothes—the too-tight summer dress and a pair of light, open sandals, not much more than flip-flops, really. I'd have been better able to race through the trees in my runners and jeans. It was too hot for clothes like that, though, once you got out of the shade of the woods.

I chased along, stumbling over roots and mossy stones. As I passed under the foresters' hut, I noticed that the door was open. I didn't have time to stop and see if Tim was about. I kept going. As I ran, I had the weirdest sensation that a scrap of violin music was streaming after me, wafting over my head.

Once I emerged from the woods, I had a flat, paved road to run on and I picked up speed. By the time I reached the bus stop in the village, I thought my eardrums were going to burst with the force of the blood pounding in my head, and every bit of me felt swollen to twice its proper size. My heart was trying to leap out of my body and my lungs hurt every time I breathed. I slumped against the cool metal pole of the bus stop, in the shade of a large sycamore tree that grew out of the pavement, and gulped huge painful breaths. When I licked my swollen lips, I tasted salt. I found a tissue and mopped my sweat-beaded face with it. I wished I had something to drink, but—wouldn't you know it?—I'd left my water bottle cooling in the stream.

Gradually my heart began to settle back into its place inside me and I could breathe at a more normal pace. Where was this flipping bus, after all that running? I dabbed the sweat off my eyelids and checked my watch. Three twenty-nine. A whole minute to spare. And where was flipping Gillian? I looked around. Not a solitary other person. July. People were away on their holidays or out in the sunshine, gardening or catching skin cancer, not waiting for a smelly, hot bus to the next town.

Here it came now. I couldn't see it yet, but I could hear the clanking, rumbling, wheezing sound it made. It sounded as if it were about a hundred and had emphysema. I was amazed that it was going to be exactly on time. It never was. Blast Gillian anyway! Where could she have got to? All that running for nothing! Didn't she *want* to find her father? I leaned against the bus stop and closed my eyes. Perspiration still clung to me. I could feel the clamminess all over my skin, under my clothes.

The bus clanked and rumbled closer and closer, the noise seeming to get right inside my body. I stayed where I was, eyes closed, waiting for the horrible, smelly, noisy, belching creature to pass me by, move on, and leave me with some peace to decide what I was going to do next.

But it didn't do that. Instead, it stopped with a shudder, though I hadn't hailed it. The engine's rumbling was worse when the bus wasn't moving, more concentrated. I opened my eyes just as the door clattered back, leaving the doorway gaping. The driver's voice shouted cheerily at me over the noise of the engine: "Well, are you just making friends with that bus stop, or are you getting on?"

"Me?" I said. "Oh, I'm just waiting for someone."

"You mean, you're not getting on? I stopped for nothing?" The bus driver pouted, pretending to be hurt that I didn't want to get on his bus.

I laughed. "Oh well," I said, without really thinking, "sure, now that you're here, maybe I'll go for a spin." I stepped up into the bus as I spoke.

"Why wouldn't you?" said the driver, and gave me a wink. I delved into my pocket and found some change.

It seemed to be even hotter inside the bus than outside in the sunshine. There was a smell of old dust and old seats and oil, and there wasn't a single other passenger. No wonder the driver had hoped I'd get on. He must be lonely.

"Ballymore?" said the driver.

"How did you know?" I asked, handing over my fare.

"That's where I'm going to," he said.

"Well then," I said, and put my hand out for my ticket.

"Sorry, machine's broken," he said.

"Well then," I said again, and sat a few seats back from the driver, close enough that he felt he had company, but not so close that I would feel obliged to talk to him. I had to think. What on earth was I doing, going to Ballymore all by myself? I'd better tell my mother. That was the deal. I could wander around Ballybeg, but if I left the area, especially if I was on my own, I had to report in by phone. I dug in my pocket again and fished out my mobile. The little screen was dead and dark. Sometimes it turns itself off if it hasn't been used for a while. I pressed the ON button and the screen flickered blue. Then it went dead again. Out of charge. I pressed ON again, harder this time. This time it didn't even flicker. Completely dead. Well then, I thought, and stuck it back in my pocket. My mother need never know, I thought hopefully, if I got home by about five as usual.

It only took fifteen minutes to get to Ballymore. The bus stopped in a small square with sapling trees around it and benches for people to sit on while they waited for the bus. I wobbled to the front and asked the driver about the time of the bus back to Ballybeg.

"There isn't one," he said. "The last bus from Ballymore to Ballybeg left ten minutes ago. Summer timetable."

A wave of panic washed over me. I was stranded in this strange town, with my phone out of charge.

"What! You drove me here, knowing I had no way of getting home again!"

The driver laughed. "Don't blame me. I don't write the timetable. Anyway, you never said you wanted to come back."

"But. . . ."

For goodness' sake. What did he think? Was I going to hitch a ride from a passing swallow, like Thumbelina?

"Well, I'm sorry, but I assumed you would make your own arrangements about coming home. I'm not in charge of looking after stray kids, you know. Who are you going to see?"

"Someone," I muttered.

"Well, I hope it's someone with a car. Is it?"

I didn't really want to pursue this conversation. I shrugged. "I s'pose," I said.

"Right so," he said, "now off you get now, young lady. I have to take this bus to the depot and then I'm off duty. Good-bye. Have a nice day."

And to think I had sat near the front, just to keep him company! Now what was I going to do? I looked around the deserted streets. An old woman came out of a grocery shop and crossed the road, her shopping bag banging against her knees. A car turned into the main street out of a side street, cruised along to the T-junction at the far end of town, and then turned right and disappeared. Two small boys came out of a house with bright pink geraniums in the window and started to kick a ball about on the footpath. This place was no busier than Ballybeg. Being so deserted made it scary, somehow. And it was horribly hot.

I started to walk down the main street, towards the T-junction, looking in the shop windows as I passed. A jewelry shop. A pub. A clothes shop, with a sheet of yellow see-through plastic spread over the clothes to protect them from the sun. Clothes wearing sunglasses! I snorted to myself. It made them look immensely dreary, all a horrible medicine color. A hardware shop. Another pub. A vegetable shop. A small cafe. A snooker place. A stationery shop. Nobody seemed to be in any of them, neither customers nor shopkeepers. Perhaps they were all sitting in the back with their feet in basins of cold water, willing customers not to come. Another pub. Even the pubs seemed empty, though I didn't actually look inside. A bookshop. A dry cleaner's. Another . . . A dry cleaner's! I stepped back to look at it. The door opened and a Chinese person came out on a blast of hot and chemical-smelling air. I smiled at the Chinese person. The Chinese person smiled back. I was ridiculously pleased to see a friendly face.

"You lost?" asked the Chinese person pleasantly.

"No," I said uncertainly. "I'm just looking."

The Chinese person smiled again. "Very good dry cleaner's," she said. "Very good."

I wasn't sure if she was the owner of the dry cleaner's, advertising her wares, or just a particularly contented customer. I nodded in a way I hoped would do for either situation. I tried to think of some way of keeping this smiling person with me. I felt safe in her company. I didn't like the eerie emptiness of the street.

"Do you know Mr. Regan?" I asked.

"Oh yes," said the Chinese person. "He lives upstairs." She pointed to a narrow door to the side of the dry cleaner's that I hadn't spotted before. It was open to catch whatever draft might come in from the street. "You his daughter?"

"No!" I said, horrified at being mistaken for Gillian.

"Hmm," said the Chinese person, and off she drifted across the street, without another word, leaving me feeling strangely abandoned. I considered calling her back, but I couldn't think what to say.

I stood and looked up at the windows over the dry cleaner's. They had aluminum frames and the net curtains seemed too big and were all bunched up at the corners. No geraniums here. The little boys with the football watched me from the other side of the street. They were grubby children. One of them had a runny nose. As I looked at them, the one with the runny nose stuck his tongue out and slurped the stream of snot into his mouth. I shuddered and looked away.

I pushed the open door a bit wider and looked inside. The hall was dark and mostly full of staircase. The stairs were carpeted in something gray or brown or maybe green or dark blue. I stepped into the hall and started up the stairs. I didn't know what I was going to say when I got to the flat, but now that I was here, I might as well press on and see if I could find this famous missing father.

I could see him as I came to the top of the stairs. The door to the flat was open and he sat at a desk under the window, with his back to me. He looked very ordinary, not a bit famous or missing. He had brown hair and he was wearing a grubby white shirt with a soft collar. He was hunched over a computer. I could hear the uneven rattle of the keys as he typed a bit, stopped to think, typed a bit more. He was certainly very tall. I could tell, even though he was sitting down, because of the way he had to fold himself up over the desk, like a penknife.

"Hello!" I called. "Mr. Regan?"

He spun around on his office swivel chair. "Who's that?" His face was porridgy. Just like someone I knew.

"It's me," I said. "Macla."

I didn't know what made me say that. It was the computer, probably, that reminded me of my e-mail name.

"You!" he said. "I thought your name was Margaret Rose."

I gasped. How could he possibly know that? Even my friends don't know my full name. I felt like turning around and flying down the stairs and out onto the blessedly ordinary street. But I stood my ground.

"Come in," he said then. "Mind if I smoke?"

I stepped into the room. It was chaotic. The desk was teetering with books and papers, the floor strewn with clothes and sticky, unwashed dishes and mugs. It stank of body and stale cigarette smoke and last week's dinner.

"It's your house," I said with a shrug, in answer to the question about smoking.

"Yeah, but it's probably a crime to smoke in front of a

child these days," he said. "You could sue me if you get cancer when you're seventy."

"You'll be dead when I'm seventy," I said. "Smokers die younger. It says so on the packet."

He grinned, and I watched as he lit a match and applied it to the end of his cigarette. He sucked and the cigarette end glowed bright red. A thin stream of blue smoke rose from it and scented the air with tobacco. I normally hate the smell of cigarettes, but it was better than the smell of the room. At least it was fresh smoke.

"How do you live like this?" I asked, looking disdainfully around me.

"Women!" he answered. "They're all the same. Wanting to tidy you to death."

Nobody had ever called me a woman before.

"No," I said. "I'm not like that. I like a bit of a lived-in look. But *this*! This place is a health hazard."

A bluebottle buzzed in angrily from the landing and settled on the rim of a plate on the floor.

"See!" I said. "It'll lay eggs, and then you'll have maggots. See if you like that!"

"You are a charming child," said Mr. Regan, leaning back in his chair. He was wearing tracksuit bottoms and his feet were bare. "Has anyone ever told you that?"

"No," I said, "because it's not true. You're being sarcastic."

"You're perceptive too," he added, dragging on his

cigarette again. "Now, what can I do for you, O Charming One?"

"You know why I'm here," I said, just like they do in the films.

"Do I? Maybe you're a health inspector? Yes, I think that must be it. Did you bring some disinfectant? Rat poison, maybe?"

"If you know my name, that means you read my e-mail," I said evenly. I was careful to keep my cool. I could see I had a slippery customer here.

"Ah yes, your e-mail. Very dramatic, I must say."

"Why didn't you reply?"

"I don't reply to every e-mail I get from a stranger. Why should I?"

"It wasn't from a stranger," I said illogically. "It was from me." I nearly lost my cool there for a sec.

"And you, my dear, *are* a stranger—to me."

"Yes, I know that, but I mean, it was really from Mir— Gillian. She couldn't send one herself as she hasn't got a computer, which I am sure you know."

"Hmm," he said, and drew on his cigarette again. "So tell me about the 'honorable purpose' for which my daughter needs 'an urgent cash advance.' Where did you learn language like that, by the way?"

"I can read," I said.

He said nothing.

"Well, she needs to go to England," I said.

He raised his eyebrows. "Indeed?"

"For an audition."

"My God! She wants to go on the stage! Her mother's daughter. Whatever makes you think that's an honorable purpose, you poor, misled child?"

"I'm not! Not that kind of audition. For a school."

"Ah!" said Gillian's dad. "So they're *auditioning* for schools these days, are they? In my day, you had to do an entrance exam. Reading, writing, sums. What's changed?"

"It's a music school," I said. *Dork,* I added silently. "The Yahooey-Manooey school. Something like that. It's world-famous. You should be proud of her."

"The Yehudi Menuhin school. My! I'm impressed. She was always pretty good on that fiddle all right. Costs me a fortune in lessons, though. And now she's looking for more cash. How much were you thinking of?"

My heart did a little leap of joy. He was coming around.

"I thought, maybe . . . a hundred?"

Mr. Regan leaned back in his swivel chair and laughed and laughed. He swiveled and laughed and laughed and swiveled. He bent his knees and pushed his toes against the edge of his desk to stop himself swiveling, but he still laughed. I stared at him, uncomprehendingly. A hundred euro wasn't *that* vast a sum, surely. He could manage that. Any adult could, if it came to it. I remembered Gillian's word: any *solvent* adult.

"What's so funny?" I asked.

"Do you know what it costs to go to that school?" he asked eventually.

"No. What do you mean?"

"I mean, it's a fee-paying school. It's very expensive. Go on, guess."

"Five hundred euro?" I asked. "A thousand? I don't know. How would I know?"

"About twenty-five thousand pounds a year," he said. "Sterling. That's more than thirty-five thousand euro. That's more than I *earn* in a year. And over five, six years, that's what? Two hundred thousand. You could buy a house for that. You could spend thirty years paying off a mortgage on it."

"Oh my!" I said. "Gosh!" I felt deflated, as if someone had let all the air out of me. I felt as if my ribs were collapsible. I didn't feel like I was in a film anymore.

"And then on top of that, you have to pay airfares, you have to buy an instrument, you need pocket money. . . ."

"Yes," I said, "I get it."

"So you see why I am amused?" He took a last drag on the cigarette and squashed it out on a plate that already had butter on it and blackened toast crumbs. "I mean, look around you, child. Do these look like the quarters of a rich man?"

Grandpa thought he was doing well, but I suppose his idea of "well" might be different from Mr. Regan's idea.

"But there has to be a way!" I said. "There must be. She's a genius."

"No, there mustn't," said Brendan Regan flatly. "Life is not like a story. You're not in *Girls' Own* territory here. No amount of valiant effort and clever plotting and having a smart and feisty heroine is going to make it possible, I'm afraid. Even for a genius, which, by the way, I doubt she is. You can't bob-a-job your way to two hundred thousand euro, Margaret Rose. And even if you could, you should probably give it to the children's hospital or cancer research or something. It wouldn't be right to pour it all into the education of one single child."

I couldn't follow the half of this. A smart and feisty heroine! Is that me? I thought. It doesn't sound like me.

"What's '*Girls' Own* territory'?" I asked, thinking of my woodland den. I wished I was there now, on my own, in the cool green shade with the stream wittering on distractedly.

"A place where things work out just because you're gutsy enough to make them," he said.

"Oh!"

"I have no intention of shelling out a hundred euro to ensure that my daughter can imprison me in debt for the rest of my life."

"No. I suppose you wouldn't want to do that."

"Right. Well then, I think that's all we have to say to one another. Could I ask you to close the front door on your way out? Thank you. I don't want any more uninvited guests. I'm busy. I have a deadline to meet." He jerked his head in the direction of the computer screen.

"Well," I said. "Good-bye." I stuck out my hand. I might as well be civil, even if he wasn't very mannerly.

He grinned and shook my small (and, I am ashamed to say, rather grubby from the bus) hand in his large, pudgy one.

"I like you, Margaret Rose," he said.

"Oh!" I could feel myself starting to blush. Smart and feisty. I didn't want to be that. I didn't want to be anything this man thought I was.

"But I'll tell you something. You need a new frock."

Who does he think he is, making personal remarks! Poor Gillian—a loopy mother and a nasty father. No wonder she's a bit odd herself!

I turned on my heel and ran down the stairs and out the front door. I had slammed it before I realized I should have left it open, just to spite him.

Gillian

It's all my own stupid fat fault. I shouldn't have mentioned it, I suppose, but I was hoping that she might just have something positive to say, my mum, and anyway, I knew I would have to tell her sometime. I do live with her; she was going to notice if I disappeared from the family for a day and a half.

"Remember I was thinking about the Yehudi Menuhin school?" I said, all casual, as if adopting a light tone was going to make any difference to how she received the news. "Well, they've invited me to an audition. Next week, actually. Isn't that good, Mum? Isn't it?"

But no, that is not good, apparently. And I know the reason why. The reason is money. We haven't got any, and Dad doesn't pay up what he is supposed to. There's hardly enough money for the ordinary bills, and there is definitely none left over for airfares.

She completely ignored me. Not as much as an "Oh?" That was hard to take. I knew there'd be an issue with money, which is why I hadn't told her the whole story in the first place, but I kind of hoped she'd put that aside even just for a moment, that she'd at least stop to congratulate me before dashing on to tell me I couldn't go.

I waited for her to react, but all she said, after a silence, was, "And how do you plan to get to this audition?"

I had just told her about the greatest achievement so far in my life, and that's all she had to say. She's not a bad person, my mother. Maddening, loopy, selfish, but not actually bad. I wouldn't want you to think that. But just at that moment, I hated her as if she was the baddest, meanest woman in the world.

"Oh," I said, as airily as I could manage, "I was hoping maybe Dad would—"

I should have known not to mention Dad.

"No," she said immediately, icily. That's all, no argument, no explanation, just a firm, nonnegotiable no. Then she added, "Under no circumstances are you to contact your father."

That was it. Again, no discussion, no argument—no audition, under no circumstances. I wanted to cry. I did cry.

My dad is selfish and my mum is selfish. Two selfish people should not get married, and they definitely shouldn't have children. People are always saying not having children is selfish. It's not true. It's the other way around. You shouldn't be allowed to have children if you are too selfish to be good at it. There should be a test for selfishness, like for blood sugar, and if your level is beyond a certain amount, you shouldn't be allowed to marry a person who also has a high level or to have children with that person. It should be against the law, and you should have to go to jail.

Mags

I wandered along the hot, deserted street, trying to decide what to do. The boys with the football had disappeared, and no one had come out to take their place. The tar was melting on the road, and little chips of quartzite in the concrete of the pavement glittered hard and sharp under the afternoon sun. The sky was so high it was hardly blue anymore, but a sort of distant white with a blazing sun like the evil eye glinting down from it. I wondered if I had enough money for an ice-cream cone. They had those instant ones with the blue paper in the newsagent's. I counted my money. If I took away my bus fare, I'd have. . . .

Then I remembered. I wouldn't be needing my bus fare, since there was no bus back to Ballybeg. I was going to have to *walk* all the way. I looked at my stupid sandals. They had pink straps. Not that the color matters, but pink does not suggest robustness, does it? When did you last see a hobnail boot in pink, for example?

I thought it was about seven miles. Maybe eight. I checked my watch. It was just after four. If I walked at a rate of two miles an hour, I would be home by . . . eight o'clock in the evening! My mother would have the police out long before that. I'd have to do better than two miles an hour. I started to trot along the pavement, still doing sums in my head. If I ran, maybe I could do four miles an hour and then I'd be home just after six. *Slap, slap* went my soft, light sandals as I jogged along. Six wasn't really all that very late.

I stopped to consider. I'd better get something to drink instead of the ice cream, in case I got dehydrated running in this heat. I went into a shop behind a set of gasoline pumps. There was a step down into a cool, shadowy interior and a smell of oranges and newspapers and motor oil. A thin collie dog raised its pointed muzzle an inch or two from the floor and flapped its matted tail lethargically at me. He looked bad-tempered but too bored to be bothered with me, so I walked carefully around him and bought a half-liter bottle of an energy drink from the fridge. I took a quick slug while the man was counting out my change.

"Hot," said the man behind the counter.

People aren't very imaginative in the things they say, are they?

When I went back out of the shop, the sun was so bright I could hardly see my watch face. I had to turn it away from the glare and bend over it to create some shade. Ten past four. I'd really better make a start.

I jogged back up to the square where the bus had come

in and started out on the road it had traveled in on. I
hoped there would be signposts all the way home. *Slap, slap*
went my silly sandals on the hard, hot road. The soles of
my feet felt hot and sore already and I'd barely started.

After about a mile, or what I thought was about a mile,
I came to a signpost. I was sweaty by now, and my tight
dress—it was tight mainly at the armholes—was starting
to dig into my flesh. I had red marks where it chafed, and
I was imagining that my feet must be beaten to a red pulp
by now.

The signpost said ten miles to Ballybeg. Was I going
backward! How could I have done such a stupid thing? I
could feel tears building up behind my eyes, tears of frustration. But the signpost was pointing this way, so I'd best
keep going. I took another slug of my drink. It had gotten
warm and tasted bitter now, but I drank anyway. Oh, woe
is me! I thought. (I didn't actually think that, but I like that
phrase, so I put it in for effect.)

I looked disconsolately in the direction the signpost
pointed. The road stretched, gray and endless, toward the
horizon, but luckily there were lots of trees, forming a sort
of cool green tunnel. It wouldn't be too hot. I started off,
hardly daring to think how long it was going to take to run
a whole ten miles.

After only a yard or two something struck me. Signposts
are in kilometers. It was ten *kilometers* home, not ten miles.
"You oaf," I said to myself, but I was laughing. "That'll be

six miles," I announced to myself out loud in my woodland voice, "or thereabouts."

I felt almost happy at this realization. Slap, slap went my sandals. The sound was starting to be comforting. Every slap a step, every step a couple of feet closer to home. The road surface here was new. It was not so sticky as in town; nor was it so flat, however. The chips of stone that had been mixed with the tar hadn't bedded down fully and made the road knobbly to run on, especially in flippy-floppy sandals not designed for such challenging conditions. But at least I had the shade of the trees now.

When I heard the whine of an engine in the distance, I kept up my steady pace, but moved over onto the verge, where meadowsweet grew up through the long grasses. The whine became a purr and then a low roar and eventually the vehicle came so close that I could feel its vibrations under my feet. I stopped for a moment on the grassy verge, my fingers playing with the creamy plumes of a meadowsweet flower, and watched the car coming closer. I'd let it pass before venturing back out onto the road again. I used the break to take another sip from my bottle.

But the car didn't pass. It stopped and the window rolled down. Maybe it would be someone I knew who could give me a lift! What bliss!

"Hey!" said a voice I half thought I recognized.

I peered at the driver, squinching my eyes to focus on him. He was wearing a red baseball cap, but he took it off when he noticed me peering, so that I could see who he was. It was the bus driver from earlier. The baseball cap must mean he was off duty.

"Want a lift to Ballybeg?" he asked. "It's on my way home."

I hesitated.

"No," I said at last. "My mother doesn't allow me to accept lifts from strangers."

"But you came with me earlier, on the bus," he said with a grin.

"That was different."

"I don't see how. A bus is bigger than a car is the only difference."

I thought about the logic of this. I agreed with him that really there was no practical difference, but I could imagine that my mother would be bound to perceive a *moral* difference. "No," I said again more firmly. "I like running."

"In this heat? You're soft in the head, you are, young one."

"Well then," I said.

"I'm a friend of your granddad's," he went on.

"Are you?" This sounded promising. Maybe it would be OK. Maybe I could take this lift.

But the bus driver had gotten tired of the conversation. "I'll give you one last chance," he said, and leaned across to open the passenger door. "In you hop now, or forget it."

I stepped forward and pulled the door toward me. My

nostrils filled with that warm-car smell—hot plastic seats and a black, enginey whiff. I slammed the passenger door shut.

"No," I said, coming around to the driver's side again. "My mother would kill me."

The bus driver laughed, jammed his baseball cap back down on his head, and revved up his engine. The tires skittered for a moment on the rough surface of the road and then the car shot off up toward the rise in the road and the horizon, its exhaust merrily blasting hotly out behind. I could hear the roar of the engine getting softer and softer as the exhaust fumes dissipated into the air, and at last there was only a whining sound and I was alone again on the road, with my half-empty and now rather sticky bottle in my hand. What kind of an idiot was I to pass up a lift? I regretted it already. (By the way, I was wrong to regret it. You should never accept a lift from someone you don't know you can trust. I knew that, really.)

I took another gulp and sighed and then I set off jogging again.

As I ran, I began to fantasize about Mr. Red Baseball Cap. I decided he was a runaway from the local facility for the criminally inclined. He'd probably stolen that bus. It was terribly old and he hadn't been able to give me a ticket. It was probably a retired bus that he'd found out the back of the depot and used for his getaway. I should have known a real bus would never have come on time. I should have been suspicious when it arrived bang on three thirty.

He was probably a child-stealer too, as well as a bus-thief, I thought, which was why he'd stopped for me at the bus stop, even though I hadn't waved him down. I was beginning to enjoy this. I gave my pet criminal a name. "Loony" Len Lafferty. Then he'd probably abandoned the bus in Ballymore and stolen a car. I couldn't work out why he was now driving back in the direction he'd come from in the first place, unless he was trying to cover up his tracks. That was probably it. Giving the police the slip. They'd never expect him to double back.

I thought maybe I should change tack and turn this into a mystery story instead of the story of me and Gillian, but I got a headache trying to work out all the reasons "Loony" Len did what he did. I had a good time imagining him trying to kidnap the two boys with the football and the snotty nose in Ballymore. That made me giggle, which is not a good idea if you are trying to jog at some speed on a hot day, so I changed then to thinking about my feet. They hurt more than ever now and my sandals were starting to chafe my insteps. I would have blisters tomorrow.

"Where were you until this hour?" my mother asked predictably as I fell in the back door, my hair clinging to my head with perspiration.

The soft flesh at the tops of my arms, where they meet my body, was smarting from my dress being tight at the armholes. My feet felt like two large hamburgers attached to the ends of my legs. It had taken me longer than I thought to get home. The heat had defeated me.

"It's nearly half past *six*," my mother was saying. "I've been demented with worry. Your phone has been dead. Mags! Answer me!"

"Sorry," I said, and slumped into a kitchen chair. "Forgot to charge it up."

"Your face is bright red. Your hair is damp. You stink! Has someone been chasing you?"

"Naw," I said. "Been running to get home on time is all. My feet are killing me."

"Good," said my mother grimly, and handed me a glass of water. "My God, Mags, you will be the death of me. I have been out of my mind. Out—of—my—MIND!"

I looked up at her. Sweat trickled over my eyebrows, making my vision bleary, but I could see that she was pale.

"Sorry," I mumbled again, and took a gulp from the glass. Water had never tasted so good.

My mum collapsed onto the chair opposite where I was sitting and lowered her head into her hands. It wasn't fair. I had tried so hard to do the right thing and I'd ended up upsetting my mother anyway. If I'd taken the wretched lift from the stupid bus driver, I'd have been home before my mother had even noticed I was gone, but I'd obeyed the asinine rules, and now look where it had landed me! (*Asinine* is my word of the week at the moment. It has nothing to do with numbers, though it sounds like it. It has to do with donkeys.)

Life is so unfair. We all have to learn this painful lesson. You are lucky to be able to learn it by reading this book, instead of having your mother practically sobbing at your feet. I can tell you that it is not a nice feeling to know you have really upset your mother just by trying to do the right thing, especially a mother like mine, who does her best, even if it doesn't always seem that way, to me at least.

"Mum?" I ventured. I stood up and put a hand on her shoulder. It was heaving horribly. I thought for a moment she actually was crying, but she was just breathing hard, in a distressed sort of way. "I'm sorry. I tried. . . ."

My mother sat up straight and swung around angrily to me. Or so I thought. But then she grabbed me, and her arms tightened around me in a fierce hug that almost knocked the breath out of me. I remember thinking, well, this is better than screaming, I suppose. Her face was pressed into my shoulder, and I could feel her breath, hot and moist as she spoke, her words muffled against my collarbone: "I could *kill* you, you stupid, careless, unthinking *brat*! Only that I love you to bits."

"Yeah, yeah," I said, pushing her away a bit, so we could both breathe. "Whatever. It's too hot for hugging." I get embarrassed by this sort of thing. If I were a proper daughter, I would fall on my mother's shoulder at moments like this, but, as I say, I am not very good at daughterhood. "Well then."

I touched a finger to her cheek, though, to make it not so bad that I had pushed her away just now. "I'm sorry," I said again.

"Oh, these things happen," my mother replied. She was calmer now. "I don't expect to know where you are every single minute, Mags, but if you are out of contact for a whole afternoon. . . . Anyway," she went on, changing into a different gear all of a sudden, "go and have a shower before dinner, and put on something clean. I can't eat with you in this state. You're snorting like a rhinoceros and sweating like a pig, your face is tomato red, and your hair is like something a bird pulled out of a hedge."

"I love you too," I said sarcastically. "You should be a poet, you know. You're great on the old similes."

My mother laughed. "Thanks," she said. "I'll keep that in mind in case the job falls through."

She had just found work three mornings a week, helping out in an office in Ballymore. She'd managed a department in an advertising company before my dad died, but she hadn't worked for some time afterward. She couldn't face it, she said. This little job was a start back into normality for her. That's how she put it. Getting back to normal. I hated that expression—as if life could ever really be normal for us again—but I knew she didn't mean it in a bad way.

When I reappeared in the kitchen, I was all polished up

and wearing deliciously clean socks, with my hair still dripping a little around my shoulders. I sat at the kitchen table and fingered my fork expectantly. I mean, it's all very well having touching little scenes with your mother, but food is still the center of family life, in my view.

"Young Gillian was looking for you," my mother announced, dishing up the spaghetti. "She rang earlier."

"When was this?" I asked.

"About three. That's when I started to worry. I thought you were with her. I told her to try your mobile, but she said you weren't answering. That bothered me, and I tried ringing you myself. When you weren't here by five, I got really worried. I was going to ring the guards if you hadn't got home by seven."

I said nothing. I'd hoped this conversation was over. Maybe if I said nothing, it might stop now.

But Mum had other ideas. "Well?" she said. "I think I deserve an explanation, young lady."

"Young lady" was usually a sign that my mother meant business.

I sighed. "I'm thinking of one," I said.

"Oh, Mags, can't you just tell me what happened? Where were you all afternoon, who've you been with, what are you up to?"

I sighed again and jammed my fork through my spaghetti. "I'm not 'up to' anything. I could have been home ages ago, if I'd accepted a lift from the bus driver. But I thought you wouldn't like that," I said virtuously, "so I didn't take it. I walked instead, all the way."

"Getting a lift from a bus driver is called taking the bus," my mother said. "I have nothing against you taking the bus if you need to get somewhere, especially if the somewhere is home. I am not *completely* paranoid."

I couldn't begin to explain. It was all too complicated and I felt terribly tired all of a sudden.

"But where were you that you needed a bus to get home?" my mother persisted.

"I'm telling you, I didn't take the bus, I walked, ran mostly."

My mother sighed. "Well, next time, take the bus, you dope. Not accepting lifts from strangers doesn't extend to not taking the bus. You must know that, for goodness' sake."

I grinned to myself. "Yes, mother," I muttered. "Lovely spag, by the way. Great sauce. I just went to see Gillian's parent," I added, deliberately slurring the t at the end of the word *parent* so that it sounded plural. No one ever uses the word *parent* in the singular, so I reckoned she would expect to hear an s at the end of it anyway.

"Oh," said Mum, cheering up. "But how come Gillian was looking for you then? She wasn't with you?"

"We just missed each other, that's all. It's a long story. You don't need to hear it all. There's nothing to it, I promise. I'll try to do better about keeping the phone charged up."

My mother gave up, thank heavens, and ladled some more sauce onto my spaghetti.

Gillian

Mags phoned me the next day. I knew she would. I was steeling myself for the interrogation.

"What *happened?*" she demanded crossly. "Where *were* you yesterday?"

I suppose I can't blame her for being cross. I had stood her up, after all, even if I didn't want to.

"I had a music lesson," I said.

A bit lame, I know, but what could I say? I couldn't go telling her that my mother had *forbidden* me to speak to my father. It sounded so stupid. It is stupid. And anyway, everything had changed now. Everything. There was simply no need anymore to go bothering Dad. We could abandon the whole Project Manhunt. So there was no point in going to Ballymore. I'd tried to ring her, to explain.

"A music lesson? A *music* lesson!" Mags was squeaking and squalling away on the phone. "*Gillian*, we had an *arrangement.*"

Sorry about all the italics, but Mags talks in italics when she gets excited.

"I know," I said. "I'd forgotten about the lesson, I got

the days mixed up, but obviously, I had to go. I tried to ring you."

"Obviously," Mags muttered, "oh, *obviously*. You *had* to go. Of *course*. It doesn't matter about a little old arrangement with *me*. *That* can be abandoned at a moment's notice, as long as Miranda doesn't miss out on her precious music lesson!"

Who the heck is Miranda? I wondered. Was it supposed to be me? But I didn't stop to ask. It probably had something to do with one of Mags's mad ideas that I didn't need to hear about. It's hard enough to follow her through an argument, without stopping to ask for explanations for all her fantasy-life nonsense as well.

"But I *have* to go to my music lessons," I said. I was getting a bit desperate, starting to talk in italics myself, but it is true—if you have a lesson, you have to go, you can't just run off to town with your friend. Though I didn't actually have a lesson, but you see what I mean, I hope. I'm speaking in general terms here. "You don't understand, do you? Nobody understands how important my music lessons are."

Now I was starting to whine. This conversation wasn't working out terribly well.

"Hmm," she said.

"I do a round trip of sixty miles twice a week," I went on, "to go to my lessons. My mother drives me."

I was babbling, I knew it. This had absolutely nothing

to do with what we were arguing about. This whole conversation was going in completely the wrong direction. I
didn't seem to be able to control it. Phone conversations
are like that sometimes. That's why it's a bad idea to have
serious conversations on the phone. The phone should be
used only for making arrangements and telling people
what time you will be home.

"Well, bully for you," Mags said sarcastically. "Look,
can we meet? I need to tell you about what happened yesterday. Your father said. . . ."

"You *went*! You went on your own?" I was flabbergasted.
This possibility hadn't crossed my mind. I thought that
when I didn't turn up, Mags would just have abandoned
the plan. I shuddered to think what my mother would say
if she heard Mags—*Mags*—had gone to beard the lion in
his den. She would never believe me if I said it had nothing to do with me.

"*Obviously*," Mags said. "I didn't have much choice,
did I?"

"Oh!" I said, thinking rapidly. "Well . . . listen, there
have been . . . um, developments. My mother wormed it
out of me that we were looking for Dad, and she *totally*
freaked out. You should see her when she does that. She's
like Tosca."

I don't know what made me say that. It was utter nonsense, but I couldn't explain what "totally freaking out" is
for Zelda. If I said there was complete silence, followed by

a chilly command that I was not to see Dad, she wouldn't have thought that was very serious. I needed to get across to her how dramatic it really was. But of course, what would a kid like Mags know about Tosca?

"Tosca?" she said.

"In the opera, you know? Where she throws herself over the balcony at the end. Tosca's her favorite opera, and that's her favorite bit, the long scream at the end. She dies, of course."

Mags clearly didn't want to admit that she hadn't the faintest clue what I was on about.

"But you haven't got a balcony," she said.

"Unfortunately," I said with a giggle.

She didn't think that was very funny. I didn't think so either. It was just a nervous giggle. She said nothing. Absolutely nothing. Was she annoyed about something?

"Mags?" I said.

"I'm here," she said coldly. "Listen, we do need to meet. I need to tell you about what your father said. He. . . ."

"Oh, that doesn't matter now," I said, trying to put her off talking about my father. It made me feel all peculiar, listening to her talking about him, after my mother had been so adamant about my not making contact with him.

"What do you *mean*, it doesn't matter?" Mags persisted, all up on her high horse now. "Of *course* it matters."

I could hear the anger in her voice. I imagined that she was probably clenching the telephone receiver with both hands, giving it a good shake between sentences probably.

"No," I said, "it doesn't. I've got the money now. I've got the tickets already. Tim's coming with me, to look after me. It's so exci— I, are you there? Mags? Hello? Have you hung up?"

"No," Mags said, "but I'm going to. Good-bye, Gillian."

And she dropped the receiver onto its cradle with such an angry *clunk* that it hurt my eardrum.

We didn't speak to each other for five whole weeks after that. Well, that's not quite true. There was one day that we half met. I mean, we were in the same place at the same time, but we didn't really speak, just exchanged a few words. Every day I had thought about phoning Mags to try and make it up, but I couldn't think what to say, and every day that I didn't phone, it became harder to think of what to say and less and less likely that I would ring her, and so it dragged on and on, day by day. And then, as I say, we met by chance at the hut. Tim was there too. It was a perfect opportunity and I was just planning to apologize and explain, but when I looked around to speak to Mags, she'd disappeared, just sloped off when my back was turned. I felt horrible.

After that, it was all much worse. Anyone can have a misunderstanding over the phone. Phone conversations are like that, because you can't see the other person's expression. But when a person just walks out on you when you're about to apologize, you feel as if you've been kicked in the stomach. That's how I felt, anyway. After that, I simply couldn't ring her. I was afraid she'd do it again. I didn't want to have that feeling again, so instead, I filled the time with practice, practice, practice.

And then of course there was the trip, and the audition and the excitement of it all. I did still think about Mags, but it was like a sore spot that you try to avoid touching, so when she floated into my mind, I shooshed her out again, and so it went on.

Mags

What happened was this.

My mother was babysitting for Lorna while Lorna's mother, Fionnuala from next door, went shopping. She'd never left the baby before, even for an hour, but took her everywhere in a little pouch thing that she strapped onto her chest. Today, though, she needed to try on some summer clothes, and she couldn't do that with Lorna fastened to her, so Mum had volunteered to mind her for a little while.

I went with her, to keep her company.

"I don't need company," my mother had said. "Lorna is company."

I glared at her.

"But of course, if you'd like to come, I'd be very glad to have you," she added quickly.

The real reason I was so keen to go with her was that I was avoiding Gillian, and I was trying to fill up my time with things that were not-Gillian. I was so cross with her about the other day, first abandoning me and then not even bothering to apologize. I felt as if she'd squashed me underfoot like a wriggling insect. I know she's older and she thinks I am a bit silly sometimes, because I'm younger, but there's no need to treat me like some sort of a *pest*.

As it happened, Lorna was fast asleep when we got there. In the daytime, she slept in a basket on the kitchen table.

"Why doesn't she put her upstairs in the bedroom?" I whispered, as Fionnuala closed the front door behind her.

"She can't bear to have her out of her sight," said my mother. "Even when the baby's asleep, Fionnuala wants to be able to see her, hear every snuffle, scoop her up at the first sign of a whimper."

"That's daft," I said.

"No, it's not," said my mother. "I was exactly the same with you. Kept you with me every minute. Couldn't bear to be parted from you. I even used to put you on the floor outside the bathroom while I whisked in to use the toilet. I'd leave the door open, in case you moved in your basket."

"Really?" I said, surprised at how touched I was to hear this. "I didn't know."

My mother smiled, but she didn't say anything more.

"Let's have some tea," I said then, "while we wait for Lorna to wake up and entertain us. I'll put the kettle on. I bet you're glad of company now. You'd be bored just sitting here looking at her, wouldn't you?"

"No, I wouldn't be," said my mother. "But I'm glad you're here all the same. Why aren't you out in the woods, though? It's another lovely day."

"Don't want to," I said. "Now, where does she keep the teabags?"

"Top left, over the kettle," my mother said. "Biscuit tin is top right. I'll get the mugs."

"What news of your friend Gillian?" Mum asked when the tea was made. "You're not meeting her today? I thought you two were getting on so well."

There she went again, trying to organize a social life for me. Before I could answer, or avoid answering, the basket on the table creaked. I looked over the edge. The baby was moving. She arched her back, stretching up her arms and waving her tiny fists in the air. Her mouth opened in a little rosy O and her eyes blinked open, deep and blue and clear.

"Oh, goody," said my mother. "She's woken. We can pick her up."

"You are a baby addict, Mum," I said with a laugh. "You really are a bad case."

My mother grinned at first, but then suddenly she turned her lips right in over her teeth, with her mouth closed, so that they disappeared altogether, and there was just a crazy line across under her nose, like a gash, where her mouth should be.

Oh, God, she's going to cry! I held my breath, as if I could stop the world by not breathing. *She's trying not to cry.* Time kept creeping forward. I knew, because I could hear Fionnuala's kitchen clock ticking, ticking. I had to say something; I couldn't go on never saying anything about the saddest thing.

"I'm sorry," I whispered.

My mother shook her head, but still her mouth was a crack across her face with no lips.

Until the saddest thing had happened, we had had something to look forward to together, me and Mum, something that kept us both linked to Dad. And then. . . .

The saddest thing was that my mum was going to have a baby, but then, two weeks after my father died, it just got washed away in the night. All the upset and shock and grief had made my mother so sick, she'd said, she couldn't hang on to the baby. She just didn't have strength enough for two. That was the saddest thing. We never even knew if it was going to be a boy or a girl. That made it worse, somehow, not knowing if it was going to be a boy or a girl. It's not the very saddest thing of all—that's not having Dad anymore—but in a way it was the worst thing, because it made everything else even sadder than it was already. That's why I call it the saddest thing.

"I mean," I went on, "I mean that I'm sorry about what I said the other day, when Don was here. I shouldn't have said it. I meant it as a joke—sort of. But I shouldn't. . . ." I trailed off. Maybe I'd said too much already. Maybe I was making it worse, by reminding Mum of what I'd said that day.

There was one of those awkward moments when nothing seems to happen. The clock ticked on, like a clock in shock, its hands to its face in horror. *Tut-TUT*, it seemed to say. *Tut-TUT*.

My mother relaxed her mouth and her lips reappeared, to my relief. Then she gulped down the rest of her tea, pushed her mug aside, and leaned over to lift the baby, who was just starting to whimper, out of her basket.

"She's too hot," my mother said, not really to me. "I think she's too hot."

Lorna smiled at my mother as she unwrapped her from her sleeping shawl and put her down on it to kick. A little dimple appeared in one cheek when she did it.

"Look, Mags," my mother whispered. "She's smiling. She's not old enough to smile, but she's doing it, look! For us."

"Bloody marvelous," I said. "I think she's going to turn out to be human. That'll be such a relief to her mother. She'll turn out a fine daughter and be a comfort to Fionnuala in her old age."

My mother turned to me then and looked right at me. There were tears in her eyes, but my nonsensical patter had made her smile all the same.

"Oh, Mags," she said, and her voice was all choked up.

Flummoxed, and feeling tears starting in my own eyes, I looked away.

"Durn mugs," I said, gathering them and the teaspoons

and moving to the sink. "Better wash 'em up before the lady of the house gets back, eh?"

I left Mum chatting to Fionnuala when she got home, and took a walk in the woods. I felt as if my brain were boiling in my head. I could do with a bit of soothing shade.

I sat for a while on my table rock in the clearing, dangling my feet in the miserable trickle that was all that was left of the stream in this heat. I noticed the depression I had dug by the rock only a few days before, meaning to create a cool place for storing food. It looked like something I had done years ago, in my distant childhood. I couldn't imagine myself now ever using it. This whole place, though it was pleasant enough, didn't seem to belong to me anymore. After I'd dried my feet on my handkerchief, I tried crawling into the tunnel I'd made, but the ferns and scrub had grown quickly in the hot weather and had closed over from lack of use. I felt grumpy, as if I'd lost something important, but I didn't know what it was. I blamed Gillian for whatever was wrong, though I knew that wasn't really fair.

I picked myself up and started to wander home. As I went by the foresters' hut, I glanced automatically upward. Tim waved to me over the low balcony of the porch.

"Watch you don't fall over," I called up to him, "and come to a sorry end, like Tosca."

"Tosca!" he snorted. "No chance! Come up and have a cup of tea with me?"

"I will burst if I have another cup of tea," I shouted, "but I'll call up to say hello."

I liked Tim. There was no need to fall out with him just because his sister was a conceited brat.

As I set my foot on the bottom wooden step, I fancied I heard a snatch of violin music. It reminded me of the day I'd been meant to meet Gillian. I'd imagined I heard violin music that day too. I skipped up a few more steps, and it came again. Not anything I recognized, not really music, just notes, seemingly random. I hesitated. I didn't think I was imagining it anymore. Gillian must be there. Still, I'd accepted Tim's invitation, so I carried on up the steps.

Tim met me at the top and threw his arms open. For one awful moment, I thought he was going to sweep me up into a giant hug. I didn't think I could cope with that, but it turned out that he was just ushering me dramatically through the door into the dark and resinous interior of the hut. I expected it to be cool in there, because of the dark, but the little wooden hut seemed to soak up the sun and instead of the fresh and delicious cave I expected, the air was thick and heavy, almost as if you could touch it.

"You're not sitting in here in this heat, are you?" I said to Tim.

"No," he answered. "I've been out on the porch, having my tea. Gillian's in here."

I peered through the dusky air and made out Gillian, twiddling with her violin.

"I thought you couldn't play in here," I said, even though I wasn't supposed to be speaking to Gillian after the way she had stood me up. I was dying to know what had happened, of course—how come she'd suddenly lost interest in finding her dad and where she'd gotten the money to go to the audition after all.

"I'm not," Gillian said, as if nothing had happened between us, as if she had never let me down, as if she had nothing to apologize for. "I'm just tuning up."

She emerged from the shadows and walked past me, out onto the sunlit porch. She didn't say any more. She didn't explain. Maybe she was waiting for me to ask. I was bursting to, but I didn't want to give in. I felt she owed me an explanation. I shouldn't have to ask. She twiddled a bit more, made some dreadful scraping noises, and then she started to play, nothing interesting, just scales. She kept stopping to tune the instrument and complain that the heat was ruining the tone.

After about a dozen scales, I clapped my hands to my ears and made a face at Tim, who was leaning against the balcony.

"I can't stand it!" I mouthed to Tim.

"I know," he said loudly. "Drives me mad too. And my mother. That's why Gill has to practice out of doors. Wah-wah-wah. . . ." He sang the last bit in a squeaky violin-like voice, in time with Gillian's playing. *Doh-re-mi.*

"The first three notes just happen to be . . . ," I sang loudly, to drown out the violin.

"Wah-wah-wah!" Tim joined in, and we both laughed.

Gillian tossed her head, turned her back on us, and continued playing.

"Let's go!" I mouthed again.

Tim grinned and took my hand. Together we tiptoed down the "fairy" steps and ran away into the woods, the *wah-wah-wah* of the scales chasing us as we ran.

We stopped when we could no longer hear the tortured notes.

"I think it's safe here," Tim said, and he sat down on a fallen tree trunk. "There's no wind, so the sound doesn't carry very far. Poor Gillian. She's a nervous wreck, you know, over this audition, and my mother is making her life a misery."

I plonked myself down next to Tim. I felt very tiny beside him. "So she is going?" I asked. "What happened? How come it's suddenly all right? I'm confused here."

"It's not really all right," Tim said, "it's just that when Zelda found out that Gillian had her heart set on going, and was even planning to go so far as to track Dad down and nobble him for the money, she shelled out herself instead."

"That's funny," I said, trying to plait some fern fronds. I soon gave that up. They were too brittle. "It would have made more sense, you'd think, to let him pay for it, to insist, even, that he paid for it."

"I don't properly understand it either," Tim said, "except that Zelda and Dad have a sort of competition going on between them. They both want to be the best parent. So she probably figures that if she gives Gill the money, then she has one up on Dad. Something like that. People who used to be married have a very odd way of going on. That's the only way I can explain it. And the bonus for Zelda is that if Gillian passes the audition and gets offered a place, then Dad'll have to pay the fees. Maybe she thinks it might be fun to land him with that bill."

"So you mean your mother is taking a kind of gamble —she's paying for Gillian to go to the audition in the hope that she gets a place and then your father has to pay up? That's—"

"Horrible," Tim said. "I know. But that's the way it is. Everything comes down to money in our family. Every single thing. And it's not fair. Gillian's really a cracker on that fiddle. Her talent shouldn't be a football between our parents, but there you are, that's the way it goes. Never get divorced, Mags."

"I'm not married," I said.

Tim laughed. "I know that, Mags," he said. "I meant. . . ."

"I know what you meant," I said. "I'll keep that advice in mind. Thank you. I believe it costs a fortune, that school."

"Not really," Tim said. "It's more than Dad would want to pay, but it's not all that terribly expensive. I mean, you have to take airfares into account as well, it's not as cheap as going to the local comprehensive, you do have to budget for it, but—"

"I thought it costs thousands."

"Yes, but very few thousands for most people. Hardly anyone pays the full fees, unless they're rich. It's subsidized like mad. A family like us would only have to pay a small fraction of the real cost."

"He lied to me, then," I said, half to myself. "About the money. I wonder why he bothered."

"To *you*? You've met my dad? How come?"

"Oh, it's a long story," I said. "Tell me something. Is it true that your mother is an opera singer?"

Tim laughed again. "She wishes! She had her voice trained, she's done a few amateur productions, but you couldn't call her an opera singer, unless you were being very kind. She's a dilettante. That's Dad's word, not mine."

"Oh, I see. I thought . . . When are you off to England?"

"Day after tomorrow," said Tim, "with Pigair."

"What?"

"You know, pigs might fly, and so might we if we felt like it, but actually we prefer staying on the ground and insulting our passengers, that's more fun."

I laughed. I'd heard of them. Then I stood up and brushed myself off. I knew I should say something about wishing Gillian well at the audition, but I couldn't bring myself to do it. I was too annoyed with her.

"Well look," I said, "I hope everything . . . you know, bon voyage and all that." It wasn't much, but it was the best I could manage.

"I'll walk you home," Tim said, by way of answer.

"No," I said. "I'd rather go on my own. Give me a head start, OK?"

Tim looked disappointed, but he nodded. "OK," he said, and he gave an absurd little wave. I waved back, wiggling my fingers. Then I turned on my heel and started to run, leaving him sitting there, idly chewing the sweet end of a long stalk of grass.

I was wearing runners, and I made quick progress over the uneven ground. As I neared the foresters' hut again, I could hear Gillian's endless, boring scales searing the air. There is something terribly depressing about listening to scales. It's probably worse if you have to play them.

I stood for a moment to get my breath, and I imagined Gillian sawing away endlessly, desperate to get everything right, to make every sound perfect. It made me feel sad inside. Nothing is ever perfect. There is no such thing as perfection. How awful to devote your life to trying to achieve the unattainable! Quite suddenly the scales stopped, though, and something new seemed to float dreamily on the warm, still air. It was so delicate a sound to start with, I thought for a moment I was imagining it, but just as I reached that conclusion, the music lifted and drifted to me through the shadowy sunlight. The sound lifted again and now I could hear it quite clearly, pouring through the woods like the sunshine—soft, warm, intense, just this side of unbearable, and then, when I thought it was really going to get unbearable, something somewhere seemed to flip over an edge, and there it came again, the blackbird, swooping toward me, endlessly, delightedly swooping. It alighted for a moment on a twig, swayed briefly, and then slipped off again into the slanty air and disappeared over the treetops, and I knew what I had to do. It wasn't much, it probably wouldn't have any effect, but I still had to do it.

I closed my eyes and crossed all the fingers I could manage and I wished and wished. I wished so hard I began to see little multicolored lights dancing inside my eyelids. I'd had a lot of practice at wishing, but my wishes had never come true. I'd wished on falling stars and on blown-out birthday candles, on shiny copper pennies and at wishing wells, but nothing worked. Maybe that's because I'd been wishing for myself, I thought now. Maybe to come true a wish has to be completely selfless. Maybe you don't need a falling star, just an open heart. And so what I wished for this time was that Gillian would pass her audition and get her place in that school she seemed to care so much about. I felt so sorry for her, caught in the crossfire of her parents' constant battling, and working so hard to get this thing she wanted so desperately. She deserved it, not for being a delightful person, but for being so good at what she does best, and for working so hard at it.

When I opened my eyes again and waited for the afterimages of the dancing lights to dissolve, I saw that a blackbird sat on a branch, just at eye level, watching me. I almost gasped. It was a real blackbird, like the one I'd seen the other day, pulling the worm out of the earth. The bird stared and I stared back. Then it dipped its sleek black head, flapped its coal black wings, and rose from its branch, climbing the shimmering air. I craned my neck to watch as it swirled away into the green and leafy wood.

My mother grinned when she saw my head coming around the back door.

"We have a visitor, dear," she said in a strange, high, excited voice.

She never called me *dear*.

I kicked off my runners at the door and came into the kitchen, carrying them by the laces. A scruffy man with a red baseball cap jammed down on his head sat at the table, opposite my mother. They were drinking tea.

I opened my mouth to speak to my mother, but no sound came.

My mother said, "Mags, this is Mr. Lafferty. He is an old friend of mine and your father's, since our college days. He's not my boyfriend, so don't start on that again, and remember, do not mention prams outside supermarkets."

Horrified, I stared at "Loony" Len. He took off his baseball cap and said, "Recognize me now, do you?"

I nodded, my eyes still wide, my heart thumping.

"She's a good girl," my mother was saying to Len. "A fine daughter. I tell her so myself, but she finds it hard to accept. She hasn't got over Ben's death, you know. It's tough at her age, of course. . . ."

I couldn't believe my mother was having this conversation *about me* with this stranger. But that wasn't the main thing. What was the main thing? Oh yes, I had to warn her, somehow I had to warn Mum that this man was possibly dangerous.

"Mum!" I wailed, or tried to, but again no words came, nothing but a squawking sound, like Gillian tuning up her violin. My throat felt hot and thick, like the inside of the little wooden hut in the woods. I understood now what Gillian meant when she said she couldn't play in there, the music got all muffled. That's just what was happening to my voice.

I stared at "Loony" Len, and as I stared, little lights began to dance before my eyes, and he started to morph, very slowly, into Gillian's father.

"You're not in *Girls' Own* territory now, you know," he said, and leaned back in his swivel chair, smirking at my mother.

My mother went on grinning dementedly.

I tried to scream again. Still no sound came, but the effort threw my whole body into spasm and I woke with a start. As soon as I woke, the scream came, loud and long.

My mother came rushing into the room, snapping on

the light switch. The light hurt my eyes and I pulled a pillow to my face to block it out. My mother called, "Mags! Don't! You'll suffocate!"

Slowly, blinking, I lowered the pillow. Carefully, I looked around the room.

"It was a dream," I said, putting my hand flat against my chest, feeling my heart like a wild bird inside me. "It must have been a dream. Oh, *Mum*! I thought he was going to get you, *kill* you!"

I flung myself back on my other pillow and wailed. Tears pumped out of me and streamed down the sides of my face, soaking the pillowcase on both sides of my head. My stomach retched with sobbing. "Oh, Mum!" I wailed again, between sobs.

"It's all right," said my mother softly. "It's all right. Sit up a minute."

I sat up, still sobbing. My mother dabbed at my tear-dampened face with the corner of the duvet cover. Then she whisked the duvet off and turned it around in a flash, so the dry part was to the top. She turned the damp pillow over, put the second pillow on top, smoothed the pillowcase with both hands, and gently tipped me back onto the pillows.

"Now, stop crying," she said, "or the second pillow will get wet too, and we'll have to change the bed linen. I don't want to have to do that at three o'clock in the morning."

I managed a small grin and wiped the last of my tears with my fingertips.

"Now, I'm going to turn off the overhead light, but I'm going to put this lamp on for a bit, and I'm going to put the radio on too, for company, and then I am going to bring you up a nice cup of hot chocolate. And when you've had it, you can turn the radio and the light off and snuggle back down to sleep, but I'll leave the landing light on and the door open, and I'll leave my door open too, so it'll be almost as if I'm in the same room."

I grinned broadly this time. This exact speech was a ritual from my childhood.

"Thanks, Mum," I said, "but I think I can manage without the chocolate. It's too hot."

"All right, then, I'll bring you a glass of water. OK?"

"OK," I said. "Mum?" I was going to make an admission I'd never make in daylight hours. The dark seemed to rub the corners off familiar things and make them seem different. "I miss Teddy Murphy," I said. "I wonder what happened to him."

My mother sniggered. "You big baby, you."

I bit my lip.

My mother left the room and came back in a moment with a glass of water—and Teddy Murphy.

I opened my eyes wide with delight.

"Where did you find him?"

"Oh, I had him in my room," said Mum. "He's been

there since I came across him in the unpacking. I didn't think you wanted him anymore, and I didn't like to think of him being lonely."

"Mum! You are such an old softie!"

"Less of the old, please," said my mother with mock primness. "Goodnight, Mags."

"Goodnight, Mum."

The Happy Ending

The advice seems to be to have a happy ending, and I have no principled objection to that, so this is it. Also, it's what actually happened.

It was weeks later, I should explain. Gillian and I hadn't spoken since that day on the phone, the day she hadn't apologized, except for the few words we'd exchanged at the wooden hut, the day Tim and I ran away from her scales and had our little chat in the woods and he told me not to get divorced. I'd tried to get over it, especially after Tim had explained how awful things were for Gillian at home, but it still rankled, just a bit. I was working on it, though. I really was ready to put it behind me, if only she would just say something to break the ice. But it had turned into weeks now since we'd spoken, and it was getting harder and harder to bridge the gap that had opened up between us.

But we went along to the recital all the same, at the school in Ballymore. We weren't invited especially or anything. We only heard about it in the village. It was Mum's idea to come.

The chairs in the school hall were the stacking plastic kind that bend unsettlingly under your weight.

"How can they charge for tickets and expect people to sit on these things?" my mother grumbled. "I should have brought cushions. I don't know why you wouldn't let me. There's nothing wrong with my cushions."

"They didn't charge for tickets!" I said. "But don't say a word. I'm just too nervous. I think I'll be sick if you say anything upsetting."

My mother snorted. "I meant on other occasions, they must charge. And it's performers who're supposed to be nervous," she said, "not the audience."

"I know," I said. "But I feel sort of responsible, you know? I encouraged the idiot. Oh, look, there's Tim."

I waved, but Tim didn't see me. He was showing Zelda to a seat in the front row. She was wearing an alarming outfit consisting mainly of black satin straps, as far as I could see. The small amounts of material that were held together by the straps were also black satin. Her shoes were mostly straps too.

"That giant?" my mother was enquiring rudely. "That's your friend Tim?"

"He's not a giant, he's just tall as a tree," I said. "And he's a sweetie pie."

"Oooh, excuse *me*," said my mother. "I didn't know you two were such *mates*."

"Oh, do stop, Mum. It's not like that. Don't be ridiculous. He's *sixteen*!"

Don grinned at my mother. I suppose you are wondering what Don was doing there. So was I. I imagined he was "passing through" again. Maybe he was on the way back from wherever he'd been going the first time.

Grandpa was there too. He insisted on sitting in an aisle seat, so he could trip people up with his walking stick. I sat beside him, then came Mum and then Don.

"Now, Barbara," Don said, "I know it's tempting to give Mags a dose of her own medicine, but I think you might desist just for this evening. She's obviously nervous. You don't want to make her worse."

"Oh, look, there's Mr. Regan," I said, pointing excitedly but remembering to keep my voice down. I didn't want to be spotted. "That's Gillian's father."

"He's tall as a tree as well," my mother said.

"I didn't think he'd come," I said. "He doesn't approve of Gillian's violin. I wonder if he'll sit with. . . . Oh, yes, he's going to sit with Zelda. That is to say, Mrs. Regan. Though I don't think she calls herself that."

"I should hope not," said my mother, who'd always been a Ms. herself.

"So, what do you think of *that*?" I asked.

"I don't think anything of it. Why should I?"

"They're *separated*, Mum. They're supposed to be At Daggers Drawn! And he doesn't even want Gillian to be a violinist. He didn't approve of her doing the audition, even."

"Well, I always say, you never know what goes on in

anybody else's family. We haven't the least clue. And it's none of our business."

"It is my business, in this case," I argued. "I was the one who found him, who tried to get him to pay up for Gillian going to her audition."

"Mags, what are you talking about? What do you mean, you *found* him? Was he lost?"

"Worse," I said, through gritted teeth. "He was hiding. And he told me he didn't want Gillian to do the audition or to go to that precious school of hers, and now look at him, all smiles. I suppose he's decided to make the best of it."

"Mags! You have been interfering!" my mother said. "Did it do any good?"

"No, I'm telling you. I was sure all I needed to do was find him and then everything would fall into place. That's what Gillian seemed to think, anyway. It turned out that he was absolutely useless, worse than her mother, and that's saying a lot. I must say, he looks better when he's dressed up."

"So do most people," said Don, leaning across my mother to talk to me. "I like the new dress."

"It's not too flowery, is it?" I asked. "Only, they hadn't got any with triangles. I wanted one with triangles on it, but the people who design clothes have no imagination. It's flowers or plain. I thought plain was boring."

The dress had huge red sunflowers on a black-and-white background. And before you start objecting, I know sunflowers are supposed to be yellow, not red, but it's poetic license, I suppose.

"It's very . . . dramatic," said Don diplomatically, and hid a small smile behind his program. "Very you, Mags," he added, "if I may say so."

I looked down doubtfully at my dress. "Well, at least it's not silly," I pronounced at last.

This time Don could not suppress a snort of laughter.

"You think it *is* silly?" I said, panic-stricken.

"No," said Don, "I really do like it. I'm laughing just because it is such a Mags sort of dress. It's as if the dress company knew exactly what you'd like and made it especially for you, confident in the knowledge that you would sail into a shop one day and buy it."

I looked at him curiously. "But it hasn't got triangles," I said flatly. "Oh, look, here comes Gillian now. Oh my *God*, she looks a million dollars!"

Applause burst around the hall as Gillian appeared onstage, caught in a soft creamy spotlight, and gave a tentative little bow. She was wearing an electric-blue dress that fell softly from the shoulders and was gathered in flatteringly at the waist. Her fuzz of hair was braided tightly to her head, and tiny strands of blue silk shone among the braids. I don't suppose she'd been to Lanzarote. Someone must do it locally. I made a note to find out.

"Ladies and gentlemen," boomed a voice from the

other side of the stage. The school principal, only you couldn't see her as she had no spotlight, so the effect was rather eerie, like the voice of Big Brother. "Ladies and gentlemen, Ballymore Community School is delighted . . . this short recital . . . *blah blah blah* . . . local musical celebrity . . . prestigious Yehudi Menuhin school . . . *blah blah blah* . . . an honor . . . a magnificent. . . ."

I sighed and wriggled in my seat.

"Now, Gillian has an arduous few years ahead of her . . . *blah blah blah* . . . all looks very glamorous and exciting . . . very hard work, *blah blah blah* . . . failures and disappointments . . . achievements and accolades. What you or I might consider a breathtaking level of skill and talent is only average in the environment she is entering . . . hopes and dreams are quite a burden. . . . We all wish. . . . and we hope . . . ."

Silly old bag. Let Gillian get on with it.

The audience evidently shared my feelings, because they suddenly burst into loud applause and drowned out the principal's witterings. Gillian moved to center stage.

She bowed nervously while the audience still clapped like mad, and then tucked her violin under her chin. I couldn't bear to look while she pecked and twiddled for a moment at her instrument—but then it happened, just as I knew it would.

First the gypsy dancers came trooping onto the stage, gathering quietly and tapping with increasing impatience and finally throwing themselves into the frenzy of the dance. Firelight crackled, skirts swirled, feet clacked, until at last, with a wild flinging motion, the gypsy princess flew through the air, skirts flying, into the arms of the prince, who twirled her till she spun and spun and her hair flashed with fire and joy.

Applause drowned the final triumphant note or two, as Gillian yanked the bow across the strings and flung it out from her body and bowed, all in one swift, fluid movement.

"My goodness!" said my mother, as the applause swelled up so that the whole hall seemed to ring with it. "Good heavens!"

Gillian's little gopher face seemed to swell up to almost normal proportions as the applause thundered around her. I grinned like mad and stood up, clapping with my hands in the air.

Gillian bowed again and then she stepped forward a little, the spotlight following her. I sat down when I realized I was the only one standing.

She played a few other pieces after that, ones I didn't recognize. They were good. Everyone clapped like mad at the end of each one. Then after about half an hour of this, Gillian lowered the violin to her side and addressed the audience in a clear, strong voice.

"Ladies and gentlemen," she said, "the next piece is dedicated to my friend, Margaret Rose Clarke."

Goosebumps shot up all over my skin. I felt as if someone had just opened a freezer door as I passed by. Then the world all went red. I blinked in my darkened seat and everything I looked at glowed a dull red. I blinked again and closed my eyes. Even the insides of my eyelids were red, like theater curtains. I held my breath for a moment, waiting for those tense, delicious opening seconds of near-silence to be over, for the sound finally to grow and establish itself and fill the hall so that here in the stifling late-summer air, with people coughing gently and shifting on their uncomfortable chairs, a phantom blackbird would swoop and skim and fly through the greenwood, joy pouring from his faultless throat.

"Well done, Mags," said Don, when the applause died down.

"What!" I snapped. I felt as if I were made of something very delicate, something that might crack and fall apart at the least tap.

"I mean, congratulations on the dedication."

"I'm not her friend; she's not my friend. We are acquaintances, merely," I said.

"Well, congratulations on your remarkably fine acquaintanceship, in that case," said Don, arching his eyebrows and taking my mother's hand in his as they stood up.

I stared at their clasped hands.

"You two . . . ," I said, but I couldn't find the words to finish what I had to say. "Well then," I added lamely.

"Us two," said Don, smiling, and swung my mother's hand gently by his side.

She smiled too, unnecessarily soppily, in my opinion. Grandpa stared at them with his mouth open, but he didn't say anything, which is surprising, because he usually does say something and it is generally the wrong thing. People say I am like him in that respect. That is total rubbish.

"I think you might go and congratulate your . . . acquaintance," said my mother. "You two, you could get to be friends, with just a bit of. . . ."

I waited to hear what I needed a bit of in order to become Gillian's friend, but my mother was stumped. She looked at Don to help her out.

"Oh, I think Mags can work it out for herself," Don said, which was quite the most sensible thing I had ever heard him say. I thought he might do. "She's pretty smart. She may not be a world-class musician, but she knows a blackbird from a sausage all the same."

"And I'm sure you want to say hello to Tim," my mother added. "He looks such an interesting boy."

"Well then," I said gruffly, and turned away to walk out of the hall ahead of them in my startling new dress, my head whirling with possibilities, bright red possibilities, sunflowers of possibility, for tonight, for tomorrow, for the rest of the summer, for life, even.

The Slightly More Muddled and Not Quite so Happy Ending

You know if you open up a clock and you take all the innards out and twiddle around with them and you put them back in again, in roughly reverse order and in what you hope are the places you found them in, and screw it all back together again and then you find that there is a short spring, a thing that looks like an elastic band only stronger, and a squashed object that might or might not be a petrified bluebottle, or possibly an overcooked currant with legs, still left on the kitchen table? The clock works and ticks and everything, but what about the leftover bits? That's what this chapter has in it, the petrified bluebottles of the story. Properly constructed stories written by grown-ups who know what they are doing don't have any bits left over at the end, or if they do, the grown-ups are better at sweeping them away with a quick flick so nobody notices. But I am new to this game, and I always think honesty is the best policy, so I have decided to add in a few explanations about how the happy ending was a bit messier in real life.

Everything in the last chapter is true. Gillian did say that thing about dedicating the piece to me, and I suppose that is much the same as saying she was sorry about what a bad friend she'd been before, so I decided to forgive her, because I am a large-hearted person. Also, you have to make allowances for the fact that her parents are so awful, even if she doesn't think they are all that bad. She has to look on the bright side, doesn't she? These are the only parents she's got, so she has to make the best of them, I suppose.

It is also true that Mr. Regan did come and sit beside Tim and Zelda at the recital, but you mustn't think that because that happens at the end of the story it means they are getting back together or something. It just means that on this one very special occasion, when Gillian was strutting her stuff, they felt they should put their best foot forward and behave like a family.

You are probably wondering about the money. I wonder about that part too. Gillian's father was very clear that he couldn't possibly afford to send Gillian to that school, and then Tim casually announced it wasn't such a big problem after all. I don't know whom to believe. At least, I do believe Tim that it is not as expensive as his father let on, but I don't understand how Mr. R. can have changed his mind so radically that he is now suddenly going to let her go after all. Maybe Tim is right when he says it has to do with this competition that is going on between their parents. They are both trying to prove to Gillian and Tim that they are the nicer one, and so they are vying with each other to find ways of making it possible for Gillian to take up her place in the school, even though neither of them really wants her to go. I find that hard to believe, but my mother says that you never know what goes on in other people's families, no matter how well you think you know them.

Anyway, Gillian has just started in the Yahooey-Menooey school (I will always call it that), and I have started in my new school in Ballymore, but we have vowed to be pen pals during term time, and Tim has decided that he does like being a forester and when he has finished at school and got his Leaving Cert and all, he is going to study forestry.

Lorna has a tooth, which is unheard of at her age, and which proves of course that she is ridiculously advanced and will probably be an inventor or a rocket scientist when she grows up.

"Loony" Len doesn't exist. At least, he does, but he's not loony and he's not called Len. He is a proper bus driver. He drives the school bus in term time. I am very haughty when I see him, because of that time he never told me about the summer timetable and I had to walk ten miles home. (Miles are more dramatic than kilometers, aren't they? I wonder why.)

And my mother. You mustn't think just because she and Don were holding hands that evening, that they are going

to get married or anything. It just means that they are getting on very well at the moment, and you never know. You
never do know anything, really, about anything until after
it has happened, and even then you don't know much
either, which is why life is so confusing and why books are
usually better than life, because in books, it is the author's
job to make things less confusing for the reader.

The other thing you may be wondering about is how I
feel about Don and my mother maybe getting together.
Mum said the thing is not to think about it as having anything to do with Dad. She says this is a separate thing, and
it doesn't affect how she feels about Dad or about me, and
even if she did decide to marry Don, Dad would always be
her First Love and he would have a special place in her
heart and all sorts of palaver like that that made me want
to cry, including stuff about life must go on, which sounds
to me as if she is going to marry him after all, even though
she says she isn't, or not just yet, anyway.

I have decided that I am not going to worry about it for
the moment, because it might not happen, and even if it
does, by the time it happens, I may have gotten used to the
idea. The main thing is, Don is OK. He's not specially
good at playing Frisbee or fishing or putting on funny
voices or remembering the exact amount of milk you
like in your tea or any of those things a dad is supposed
to do, but then he says he is not trying to be anyone's
dad, which is fine by me. He makes the most fantastic

brownies, though, which is a definite plus, because Mum never makes anything fattening.

I think that is everything, except for Grandpa, who is the same as ever. He says isn't it just as well he didn't move in with us, because now look, whatever that is supposed to mean.

GAYLORD RG